THE SCREAMING DEAD

PETER MARK MAY

AND

RICHARD FARREN BARBER

Macabre Ink

They lined themselves up as best they could and set off into the darkness, arm in arm. The ground underneath was level and had no grass or debris underfoot. They could not hear, see or feel anything. They took every step with a nervous trepidation, wondering if the ground would still be there, or if a black abyss would send them tumbling into the darkness.

Paul tried to think of his brother and the near telepathic thoughts they shared when they were both alive. Maybe in death that would return. Paul wished it so, like a prayer. He thought of his twin brother, conjuring his face in his mind's eye. It was difficult to pull his image from his mind. The surrounding darkness did not help. It conjured up primal fears of what monsters the world may hold.

Paul blinked five times in a row, just to make sure his eyes were open. A long distance ahead there was a smudge of light in the darkness. Paul blinked five times again, wondering if it might be some neural flash on the back of his retina.

"I see something," François whispered. He sounded scared.

Paul felt the hairs on his neck and arms go rigid, like a cold breeze had blown over them.

To his right, Cookie hissed. "I see it too, it's coming closer, and fast." Her grip on Paul's right hand tightened until it began to hurt.

The football-sized object raced towards them at breakneck speed.

The pale thing came closer, until they could make out the glow of a small face.

No, not a face, but a white, eyeless skull.

A Macabre Ink Production — Macabre Ink is an imprint of Crossroad Press.

ISBN 978-1-952979-75-0

For information address Crossroad Press at 141 Brayden Dr., Hertford, NC 27944
www.crossroadpress.com

First Edition

CHAPTER ONE

The first thing Sam noticed was the silence. It came before the darkness and the stillness. It was complete. It did not sneak in underneath the sounds of the world. It was simply there; fully formed, as if this was how his life had always been.

He strained his hearing to find any noise; the sound of a child playing out in the yard or the call of birdsong or even just the wind rustling through dead tree branches, but there was nothing.

Sam opened his mouth, preparing to say something, but he realised he had no idea what he wanted to say and pressed his lips together. He understood that he was too afraid to say anything because of the chance that no one would respond.

Instead, he opened his eyes, or at least tried to open his eyes. They were already open. He closed his eyes, and opened them, and closed them. It took him a few minutes to accept that it made no difference; he was blind. Blind and deaf.

He put his hand up to his face to test how complete the darkness was, but before he was able to touch his nose his fingers brushed against something. The material beneath his fingertips was soft. He reached out with both of his hands to explore the area in front of him. The cloth was smooth and he tried to decide what it reminded him of. He had a memory of a school classroom and he imagined he must have been no more than five or six years old. There was a pit in the corner filled with sand and water that they were only allowed to play in if they'd finished their lessons. There were scatter cushions around and it was something familiar about the cushions.

It came to him slowly. He didn't consider himself the brightest guy in town, but it had never felt so hard to think before. Every thought in his head had to be forced into existence.

The cushions. Something about the cushions. He remembered the colours: bright red and bright blue and bright yellow; there was no room for anything muted or subtle in the classroom. The cushions had been slick, which was what he remembered about them. Slick and shiny.

Like silk.

Sam brought his hands up again and inspected the material with his fingers. That's right, silk.

He pressed into the material, his hands enfolded by the silk. Finally, his fingers stubbed against something harder. He pushed against this new surface but it was like he was pushing against a brick wall. His fingers scrabbled against the surface like a cat scratching at the ground. The silk protected his fingers but prevented him from getting any traction on the harder material, even when he gathered bunches of the silk into his fists and tried to rip it free.

He dropped his hands back down by his sides, his muscles ached from working in such a cramped space, and that was when he realised he was lying down.

He placed his hands palms-down by his side and tried to push himself into a sitting position. The pain that shot through his body was immediate and overpowering. He bit down on the need to scream, but it rattled through his body anyway.

The silken material was beneath him. What did that mean? He was lying on a bed somewhere?

Am I in hospital? Sam thought. The words trickled slowly through his mind and he had to construct them into a viable sentence. *In hospital, that must be it.* He tried to recall his last memory but there was nothing. Nothing at all. He had come into existence in this dark, silent place and although he knew that wasn't true, although he knew that there was a before, he had no idea what it contained.

He'd had an accident and now he was in hospital and although he couldn't see or hear, the doctors would be looking after him and soon they would work out what was wrong with him and be able to treat him.

It didn't feel right. It didn't feel true.

He tried again to rise and this time he was able to lift one shoulder. He tried to turn on his side. The silk rustled beneath him and he stopped.

I'm not deaf, he thought. The smile came back just for a moment: *I can move and I can hear.* Just the effort of trying to roll onto his side exhausted all the strength in his body and he rolled onto his back once more to rest. He lay there with his eyes open, staring into the perfect blackness, and explored the area around his hands, the silk and the hard surface beneath the material.

When the fatigue had faded from his limbs, he tried again to roll onto his side. His arms and legs trembled with the effort as he threw himself to the right, and this time his whole body lurched.

His shoulder banged into the hard edge beneath the silk and knocked him back flat on his back. *What was that?* Sam thought. He reached his hands out and followed the confines of his prison. The hard surface was not just above and below him; it was on either side, like a box.

A box. The thought almost tumbled from his mind. *Not a hospital bed. A box. A silk-lined box.*

And Sam realised why the silence was so eerie. It was not just the absence of any external sounds, it was the absence of *all* sounds. Because he wasn't breathing.

In perfect silence, Sam Wright began to scream.

CHAPTER TWO

The jagged scream pervaded into his dreamlike state, waking him. This was unprecedented during the Dreaming. He'd been woken by other people before, but never like this.

The scream had not emanated from where he was or from the lips of any of the souls that resided there. No, this came from outside this realm—from another place—but that was impossible. Paul's eyes flicked open and he could see the carved grey stone mere inches above his reclined head. The stone was hard against his limbs and not for the first time he wondered why he couldn't line the space with a soft material; cotton or maybe silk. Something to keep his bones safe. He took a deep breath—exhaled—and then swung his legs out of the man-sized oblong alcove. He had to duck his head and fling himself down onto the floor below. It was hard and jarring to his knees, but pain was an old luxury. His alcove was three rows up—one of the highest. Another figure was already climbing up the cool stone façade to replace him.

Paul turned and nearly stumbled on the rubble of rock, sand and stone that littered the mosaic floor of the crypt. The sky above was steely blue and smooth with no clouds, sun, or moon to spoil the view. He knelt down to the lowest of the alcoves, where powdered bones coated the surface, and shook the shoulder of the ponytailed man who lay *Dreaming* inside.

The man awoke immediately, and only years of experience prevented him from jolting upright. "You woke me up, you fuck-er," he said in a heavy French accent.

"I heard a scream in my dream, François, it woke me up." Paul waddled back on his haunches as his friend pulled his legs out of his alcove and sat on the edge, his arms resting on his knees.

"So?" He gave a Gallic shrug. "All my dreams are filled with screams. During my life I married three women."

"Oi, Frankie the Fork, get out of it." A large haystack of a man was standing at the head of the line of people waiting on the steps leading down into the crypt.

François clicked his right thumbnail off the top set of his front teeth. The bald, big-fisted man advanced the last two steps down onto the mosaic floor. Paul tugged his friend up by the left arm and pulled him back from any confrontation. Paul smiled at the big man. "Do you want to miss your *Dreaming*?"

The man hesitated, and Paul gripped his friend's shirt and pulled him towards the other set of stone steps.

"Why do you have to antagonise people?" Paul asked as they followed the steps up along a flat trench of walled stone.

"It helps pass zee time," François replied. "So, tell me about this all-important dreamy scream."

"It ... sounded like my twin brother screaming for help; screaming for me." They walked side by side up carved steps to a flat area of stone. Fallen walls, tombs, crypts and houses of the dead—cast in grey-blue—lay ahead as far as Paul could see. A chapel towered over everything, dominating the landscape. It had Greek and Roman pillars in front and reminded Paul of a school trip to the British Museum in London. Just looking at it made Paul feel tiny.

"But you can't dream of the living," Paul said.

François had a look of pity on his thin face, behind his long moustache and stubble. "He must have transcended." Paul kicked at a nearby rock and it rolled away and down into a deep grave. "I have to help him through this, he's my twin brother."

"It could be some messed up dream, mon ami." François clapped his right hand on his friend's shoulder.

"I know it was him. I have to go back and find out." Paul climbed up another set of flat tomb lids that had been piled on each other into steps. "You coming?"

"I don't have much else to do, eh," François replied and ran lightly up the steps in his boots and joined Paul on the walkway above. Tomb lids lay from crypt to walls to gravestones, making a thoroughfare through the graveyard in all directions. It was rare to see even a patch of grass here as they walked east to Paul's place.

"You know, even if he is dead, it does not mean that he will be here, Paul," François said. He walked one foot after the other on a thin crumbling wall to the next crypt, his arms outstretched like a trapeze artist. "We are only here by chance ourselves."

"I've got to check, Frankie," Paul said hurrying forwards at an almost-running pace.

"Don't call me that … not you," François said, jumping down to land on a patch of bare earth. Paul was just in front of him, looking down.

Paul didn't answer. He stood looking at the freshly dug grave next to his own. The gravestone was fresh and clean, unlike everything else in this place. François read the inscription over Paul's shoulder, as his friend began to cry.

Samuel Franklin WRIGHT
beloved son and brother of Paul
may he find peace at last

CHAPTER THREE

When Sam paused for a moment, it felt like his screams continued, trapped inside the plush coffin with him. He pulled at the silk that lined the box and grabbed a handful of the material in his fist, but all it revealed was the smooth wooden lining of the box beyond.

As his own screams died away, and the silence threatened to return, he thought he heard a sound.

"It's not possible," he said. He cocked his head to one side and listened. At first there was nothing, a perfect silence not even broken by the sound of his own breathing or the rush of blood through his ears.

And then the sound rose again; far away, like a noise heard through water. It sounded … Sam tried to identify the sound, but it was so faint that it was impossible to guess what it might be. Still, it was a noise, a real noise. Not just something that his imagination had produced. He began clawing at the folds of silk above his head until his fingernails scratched against the wooden underside of what Sam had come to accept had to be the lid to his own coffin.

He balled his hand into a tight fist and tried to smash at the coffin lid. There was no room to move his shoulder, and so all he managed was a few feeble taps on the underside of the lid.

He stopped. Pushed himself up and pressed one ear against the wooden panel.

Voices.

Was that even possible?

He rapped his fists against the underside of the coffin. "Hey, under here. Somebody, help me!"

He tried not to think about the last time he had seen a coffin. He could still remember the squeal the screws had made as they had been fastened shut. That was what he was up against—not just the lid but the brass screws along the length of the lid. And then, if by some miracle he did manage to get through the lid of his coffin, he had to contend with six feet of soil.

"It doesn't matter. What else are you going to do? Lie here and wait?" Sam told himself. Wait for what? For the wood to warp and crack? For earthworms and maggots to come in and feast on his body? For the roots of trees to burrow down and slip into the spaces between his ribs?

How long was all that going to take? Weeks? Months? Years? He knew he should have paid more attention in biology, but the only part of the syllabus that seemed relevant had been the sex education classes.

He laughed. The noise rolled around the inside of the casket.

The blade of a shovel crashed through the lid and almost buried itself into his head. A shaft of grey light slipped off the blade. Sam raised his hands to his face. His knuckles scraped on the metal. The edge of the blade stopped maybe five inches from his nose. Black dirt—grave dirt—fell from the hole. A shower of soil fell onto his face and into his mouth. It tasted old, as if he was swallowing a dead body.

"I got us one," someone shouted.

A fresh shower of dirt fell onto Sam's face. The blade of the shovel twitched and retracted, and Sam started to remove the splinters from the gap above his head. He could see movement through the thin wound.

Someone shouted, and before Sam had a chance to understand what had been said, the shovel punctured the lid of the coffin once more. This time the blade stopped just short of his knees.

"Hey, guys, I'm in here," he shouted.

The blade punched through the lid again. Slashes of grey light provided enough illumination for Sam to see the ivory silk lining on which he lay.

He was wearing a suit. An honest-to-goodness suit. The collar was pulled too tight around his throat, but whoever had dressed him probably thought that he was beyond the need for comfort. He inspected his hands in the grey light—the skin was pale and wrinkled.

"I'm dead," he whispered. "If they've dressed me up like a fucking dog's dinner, then I'm proper dead."

The coffin rocked around him. More black soil fell onto his face.

"Easy, fella."

The coffin lurched and Sam pressed his hands out to steady himself. Even so, his body slid toward the bottom of the coffin. His feet touched the base, and he was raised into a position that was not quite standing. At least, not yet.

For a third time, the blade of the shovel punched through the coffin lid. Two fingers hooked through the slash and began to pull at the splintered wooden remains. Two fingers quickly became four, and then the hole was wide enough for the knuckles of a hand to pass into the cavity. Whoever was out there began ripping at the coffin lid.

And that was when Sam realised he was afraid of whom had come to rescue him.

CHAPTER FOUR

They borrowed a pickaxe and a spade from Billy Botley. He sat on the grey wall swinging his stunted legs and whistling a tune Paul did not recognise.

Paul was deep in the grave now, hard stony walls surrounding him. The spade had broken through the coffin lid in several places. He passed it up to François before reaching in with his hands. He ignored the splinters of the casket lid that lanced his fingers as he pulled at the straining wood. It broke suddenly, sending Paul rocking backwards.

He threw the pieces behind him and peered through the gap in the top half of the coffin lid.

All he saw was the ripped silky linings.

His brother's coffin was empty.

Paul remained straddling the unearthed coffin, his head inches from the broken hole. He couldn't move. He couldn't think. He just kept his prayer-like position and wept for his dead twin brother.

"What did you find?" François was kneeling on the hard stony ground on the left-hand side of the grave.

"Told you he wouldn't be there, didn't I?" Billy shouted from his position on the wall.

"Compassion is not your strength, is it, William?" François shot back with a glare.

"Nor is being a fool, Frankie the Fork." His smile twisted his large lips into something more sinister. "You lose twice today. One Dreaming session for the loan of my tools and another for the empty coffin. Not a bad day's work at all." The smile returned to the dwarf's face.

"You don't have to be such a *prick* about it," François spat back. He turned his attention to his sobbing friend, prostrated on his brother's empty coffin. "There was only a slight chance he would be there, Paul."

"Slight chance?" Billy scoffed, jumping down from the wall to waddle over and collect his spade and axe. "No chance at all if you ask me. The odds of your brother dying in an accident and coming to this afterlife are so remote they aren't worth calculating. He could have died in his sleep, been murdered, or died in war. All these deaths would have sent his soul elsewhere. Then again, if it was suicide, then his soul is anyone's to claim." The little man picked up his axe and his shovel.

Paul sat up on the coffin and wiped away his tears. They left streaks of dirt on his face and his hands. He took a deep, hollow breath and scrambled out of the grave and turned to sit cross legged on his own grave. He looked from the mound of earth behind François to Billy who was wandering off with the spade and axe over each shoulder.

"How do I find out which afterlife?" Paul called after the retreating dwarf.

"Eh?" Billy turned half of his body and looked at Paul over his left shoulder.

"How can I find out where my brother's soul went?"

"How should I know?" Billy shrugged. "I just dig the graves. I have nothing to do with how the bodies get there."

"But you have been around since the old gods were renounced for the new one. You must have heard something in all those centuries?" François pleaded with the retreating dwarf.

"Too many things. Things that would scare you to death if you weren't dead already." Billy stared at Paul, taking in the loss etched over his forever-young face. "What would you do if you knew?"

"Find him."

"And risk your own soul?" The dwarf stared into Paul's eyes, looking for truth in the young man's words. "This is a cold place with grave built upon barrow built upon the tombs of the accidental dead. But even so, other places are not so safe. If the Great Cremator gets hold of your soul, you are lost forever."

"He was my twin brother; I'd risk anything to make sure he is safe."

Billy Botley chewed at his large bottom lip, his silver-grey eyes half closed in thought. "If you want to know how your brother died, you'll have to seek out an Augur."

"Where do I find one?"

"I'm not a travel guide, only a bloody grave-digger until Ragnarok frees me from this toil." Billy turned and jumped down into the remains of a broken tomb.

"That was some help and no help," Paul said.

"Not entirely, mon ami," François said from where he knelt next to the open grave.

"You've heard of these Augurs then?" A little hope returned to Paul's shaky voice.

"Yes." François nodded, before getting to his feet and dusting down his clothes. "You forget I have been here almost two hundred years longer than you—I know many things."

"Where are they then?" Paul asked as he untwisted his legs to stand up.

"They hang around in the catacombs under the Great Chapel in the Roman Quarter."

"Then what are we waiting for?" Paul went around his brother's empty grave to stand next to his friend.

"It's a long way to travel."

"Have you or I better things to do with our time?"

"Point taken." François nodded and pointed the way.

CHAPTER FIVE

When the coffin lid was pulled away, Sam turned his head against the shower of soil. Black dirt covered his face and he clawed it away with his hands. He jumped to his feet and the wood creaked beneath him.

Three faces peered over the edge of his grave.

"We got one, a live one."

The voice came from a small boy with a grubby face. He moved closer to the edge of the grave, pushing a new landslip of dirt down onto Sam.

"Let's get a good look at what we got here," a woman said.

Sam felt like a prize bull at a farmer's market, or a fish hanging on the end of a line. If he didn't pass the test, what would happen? Would they throw him back in? Push him down into the grave and cover him with the lid and six feet of dirt?

"Thanks," he tried to say. His mouth was still full of soil and he spat it out onto the silk lining of his coffin. "Thanks for pulling me out."

"Nothing to say thanks for yet," the boy said. "We haven't decided if you're a keeper or not."

The top of the grave was just a few inches above Sam's head. He reached out his hands and grabbed at the ground. The boy picked up a spade and brought it down on Sam's fingers.

"Hey, kid!" he pulled his hand back and looked at the man.

Sam tried again. He put his hand over the edge of the grave and grabbed a clod of grass and tried to haul himself up. From the corner of his eye, he caught sight of the third person moving forward and just had the presence of mind to let go and fall back into the grave before the old woman buried a garden fork in the spot where Sam's hand had been.

"Looks like we got us a live one this time," she said.

"What the hell are you trying to do? You could have ripped my hand open."

"Ought to be more careful then."

She was old. Ancient. Sam blinked against the slate-grey light that poured into the grave. The woman looked like she might have been alive when Jesus was a boy. The lines on her face were thick and her skin looked tough as sunburned leather. Her shock of white hair was a mass of strands that looked like wiry candyfloss.

"Help me out here," Sam said.

"You got to promise first," the boy said.

"Promise what?"

"Promise you ain't gonna cause us any trouble?"

Sam nodded.

"No, you gotta say it."

"I promise."

"Cross your heart and hope to die?"

Sam laughed. He couldn't help it. The sound hurt his throat and he remembered the too-tight tie around his neck. His funeral clothes.

He drew a cross over his chest in a motion that took him back to being eight years old, playing in the woods with Paul. The pair of them building a den. "Cross my heart and hope to die," he chanted.

The two adults looked down at the boy.

From his position at the bottom of the grave, Sam realised that he was looking up at the two grownups as if he were a child again.

He eyed-up the far side of the grave. If he ran, he might just be able to make it. He couldn't see beyond the lip of dirt, so it was impossible to tell what was out of sight, but maybe it was worth the risk.

The silent conversation continued between the child and the adults. Sam held his tongue. What the hell did they have to spend so much time thinking about? He was stuck in the grave;

they could pull him out or leave him—surely there wasn't that much to be considered?

"He might do," the boy decided.

Sam held out his hands before they had a chance to change their minds. The man grabbed him by the wrists and pulled him up. He was a scrawny-looking thing—no muscle on his bones—and yet he lifted Sam off his feet and out of the grave as if he weighed nothing more than a bag of sugar.

Sam kicked his toes against the wall of the grave to gain a foothold, and once his hips were level with the edge of the grave, he scrambled to pull himself free of the hole. He lay down on the dirt, staring up into the sky.

None of the clouds moved. Sam wasn't sure why he should notice that when he had just been rescued from his own coffin.

"Thanks," he muttered.

The boy moved closer until he was peering into Sam's face. His breath tasted of black soil, earthworms, and maggots. Sam looked at him more intently and wondered how long he had been dead. Long enough, that was for sure.

"He belongs to the Creator, just like the rest of 'un," the boy said.

Sam pulled himself to his feet. He was aware of the deep hole beside him with the broken remains of his coffin lying at the bottom.

His plot was halfway up a hill. Below him, the land was filled with gravestones. The cemetery stretched off as far as the horizon, the whole world given over to house the dead. Small headstones and large mausoleums. Angels and crucifixes and anything that the human imagination could invent, all chiselled from stone and marble. The graves were packed closely together with thin paths running through them like veins.

"I know this place," Sam said.

"Sure you do."

There was a wall off to the left. A wall of rough bricks that cut off the rest of the land from view. He couldn't see the cemetery beyond the wall, but he knew it continued. Because he'd been there before. He remembered standing in the shadow of the wall. Except…

He turned a full circle. "This isn't right."

"Of course it's not."

At the top of the hill was a stone chapel. From a distance it looked as small as a dollhouse.

"It's not right," Sam insisted.

"Can I tell him?" the woman asked.

The boy glared at her. "He needs to figure it out for himself."

"I remember," Sam murmured. They had taken a path down the side of the hill and his mother had said something trite about what a lovely view it was. As if that made a difference, as if anyone cared about the view when they were six feet underground.

"It was on the other side of the wall," Sam said, and the boy grinned.

"What was?" the old woman asked.

"Where they buried him. Where they buried my brother."

"Ahh, but you're among us now," the man said. He rubbed his hand across his throat, and to Sam the gesture was more than an idle movement.

He touched his hand to his own throat and remembered the soreness that had haunted him when he had awoken. It was still there, just like the ache at the back of his neck. And then it all made sense. All of it. The coffin. The grave. The cemetery.

"I did it," Sam said. "I killed myself."

CHAPTER SIX

"How does it do that?"

"Do what?" François asked, struggling up the side of the tumbledown pyramid to stand at the top with his friend.

"Get smaller as we get closer." Paul pointed to the bone-white chapel on top of the hill, still miles before them. "Shouldn't it get bigger?"

"You are thinking too much like the living world, my friend." François gesticulated wildly with both hands. "This is the afterlife of accidents; everything is cock-eyed here."

"How can we tell if we are making progress?" Paul waved his right hand towards the marble chapel on the hill. "How long will it take to get there?"

"My lord, you speak like a fucking infant sometimes." François turned and punched Paul, not too lightly, on his right upper arm.

Paul staggered a little which added embarrassment to the rising anger in his throat. "I only asked a fucking question, Frankie. There's no need to be such a garlic-flavoured tart about it."

The two friends stood apart, staring at one another intently for about ten seconds, their anger simmering. Frowning, they both turned to face the only edifice in the great graveyard above two storeys tall. The hill itself was not made of rock; they could see that from this distance. It chilled Paul to the bone. Even François, who had journeyed to it three times before, was silenced by it. It was forged of old bones, skulls, and torsos and had gravestones and tombs layered like some necrophile's pleated idea of heaven. The white marble chapel stood lonely on top of all those bones. There were far worse places to end up after you died, but that didn't mean this place was a harp-playing, fluffy-cloud picnic.

"Come on," François said in a gruff voice. He moved off down the side of the small pyramid into a valley of death, where the hill was lost from sight.

Paul let his French friend wander on. He sucked his top lip and stared at the hill of bones. Then he thought of his brother, all alone in some place worse than this blue-toned world, and he hurried down after his friend.

They continued on in silence for an uncounted time. The necropolis was back in full view now as they hopped between the tops of hundreds of closely pressed-together tombs. The murmurs, shouts, and wails of those interned within made them quicken their pace.

"Are we there yet?" Paul asked with a wonky grin on his face as they reached the end of the field of tombs.

François looked at his friend, but smiled and then gave a slight snigger. They stopped on a sunken stone square, surrounded by the houses of the dead. They stood on each side of a remembrance cross, one foot each on top of the thin plinth it rested upon. Their arms locked around the long, thick upright of the cross. People wandered in the shadows of their hovels, talking in whispers, looking up at the brash strangers.

"You know we are dead, correct?" François peered around the side of the thick stone post.

"Yes," Paul replied raising his eyebrows. He knew what was coming—some old philosophical tripe that François liked to spout, rather than give a straight yes/no answer.

"Then do you remember telling me about that German with his cat in a box theory?"

"Schrödinger's Cat theory, yes." Paul nodded wondering where this was all leading. Somewhere abstract usually.

"Well here." François used his left hand in a claw shape and pressed it down three times towards the ground. "The cat, whether he is in or out or fucking having sex with the box, is always dead."

Paul stared at his friend, still not getting his drift.

François could see the confusion in his friend's eyes. "It does not matter if it takes an hour, day, week, or fifty years to reach the base of the Chapel Hill. We don't need to eat, drink, piss, or shit; we are dead. We get there when we get there." François gave one of his infuriating Gallic shrugs and leapt down from the cross.

"But my brother?" Paul said, jumping down to land next to his friend.

"Is dead and will still be dead whether we find him or not."

"But what if he's in danger, in one of the afterlifes where the Great Cremator is king?"

"Oh, the Great Cremator, whoooooo." François made a ghostly noise as he waved his hands by his face. "Another old wives' tale to scare you. To keep you here, the subservient dead."

"But Old Olson says—"

"—Old Olson is a two-millennia-old Viking who got shot in the back of the neck by his own son while he tried to pull an arrow out of a straw target. He's mad because he never made it to Valhalla."

"But he says he has been to many places like this, trying to find his sons. He says he saw the Cremator up close and never travelled the planes again."

"Olson Arrowneck talks out of his anus," François replied dryly. "Come on, before I get reborn and die of boredom from your endless English prattling."

Paul looked at his friend's back—went to speak—and then closed his mouth again. Sometimes it was useless trying to argue with François, he always came out with some weird stuff that would end the argument in head-scratching confusion. In the end, he followed his friend up the sloping remains of a house of the dead onto a flat garden of grey weeds and ashes urns. The chapel seemed even smaller now and Paul hoped that meant they were getting closer.

CHAPTER SEVEN

"We need to go there," Sam said.

"Where?"

Sam nodded in the direction of the wall. "The other side. If I'm still around, my brother is too. And if he is still here, I might..."

He stopped talking. The boy was laughing. He resisted the urge to slap him across the face to shut him up. The old woman was laughing too, and even the man looked like he was struggling to remain silent. Sam clenched his hands into balled fists and tried to remember what Paul used to say when they were teenagers. *Calm down, kiddo. You won't get anywhere if you just lay into them. You need to think.* He could hear Paul's voice inside his ear, soft and calm and reasonable. But then Paul always had more than his fair share of brains.

Still, he uncurled his fingers and tried to draw in a deep breath. His lungs didn't respond, but it was enough of a distraction that by the time he returned his attention to his three unlikely saviours, he no longer had the same urge to knock their heads clean off their shoulders. Paul would have been proud.

"What's so funny?"

"You," the kid said. "I never came across anyone so dumb."

Breathe, Sam reminded himself. The kid was, what? Eight years old? Now was probably not the time to start beating up on minors.

Sam looked at the old woman. "Why?" he asked. He was damned if he was going to get his answers from some snotty brat.

She shrugged and it wasn't clear to Sam if that meant that

she didn't know or wasn't sufficiently bothered to make the effort to tell him.

The man was no better. He stood there looking out across the graveyard as if he was watching something just beyond the wall. Sam looked, but the only thing visible from where he was standing was the wall, the ragged rows of graves and the small white chapel at the top of the hill. *What sort of a screwed-up family is this?* Sam thought to himself.

"If my brother is over there…" he started.

"It doesn't matter."

The boy was wearing the sort of slick grin that would have bought him a fist in the mouth in almost any pub that Sam had ever entered. There was a knowing look on the boy's face that was completely wrong for the childish features—it was an expression that was borrowed from a world-weary eighty-year-old, not a young kid.

"If your brother is over there, you may as well forget him. You're one of us now."

"And what if I don't want to be one of you?"

"Dun't matter. You already made that choice."

Sam looked across to the other side of the graveyard. "He's over there. I haven't been to his grave that often, but I remember it."

"Are you stupid?" the kid asked. He looked Sam up and down, measuring him with his eyes. "Yeah, I guess you are. I'll say this slowly so you can understand."

Sam looked across at the man, but he gave no indication that he was planning to intervene. If Sam was going to learn what the hell was going on, then the only person willing to tell him was the leery kid.

"What you're seeing…"

"The graveyard."

The boy sighed at the interruption. "That's *your* graveyard."

"Course it is. It's where they buried me."

"It ain't my graveyard."

"What do you mean?"

Another of the boy's tired sighs. Sam thought to himself that it was almost too easy to hate this kid. He used to be of the opinion that any adult who hurt a kid had to have something fundamentally wrong with them. Those news reports of mothers and fathers beating up on their kids turned his stomach. A kid was just an echo, not enough of a person to inspire violence. He was thinking he might have to revisit his ideas about that.

The boy walked across to a headstone. Sam noticed the kid did not avoid standing on the grave. In fact, he seemed to plant his feet where the occupant's chest would be, some six feet below his shoes.

"What does it say there?" he asked. When Sam didn't respond immediately, the boy pounced on the pause. "You can read, can't you?"

Sam spoke in a slow monotone. "Here lies John Deakin. Beloved Father and husband. Taken from us too early." He gave the boy a smug grin and realised that he'd regressed back to a teenager. "He used to drink in the Black Horse with my dad. His son was in the year above me at school."

The boy ignored Sam and turned to the old woman. "Can you read what it says?"

The woman almost had to kneel on the grave before she could start reading. "In loving memory of Ethel Houghton."

She carried on speaking, but Sam didn't listen. They were making fun of him. He didn't know why—maybe death was so boring that they needed something to keep themselves entertained; it didn't look like Sky Sports covered this part of the world. And yet…

The woman was still reading from the headstone—a list of children's names and ages. Robert died at the age of 5, Nathaniel only managed 18 months.

"Your turn," the boy said. There was something about the way the man shuffled forward and took the place of the old woman that suggested to Sam that this was not the first time they had done this routine. It was just a little too slick, too rehearsed.

"Frank Hamilton," the man read. "1901-1923."

There was an eager sneer on the boy's face. "You get it yet?"

The same gravestone, three different inscriptions. Sam shook his head and hated himself for taking part in whatever game they were playing. "You're making it up."

The boy dragged his finger across his chest twice. "Cross my heart, hope to die, stick a needle in my eye." He moved forward and almost pushed the man out of the way so he could get to the grave. "Francis Jackson," he read. "You don't need to know the rest. It doesn't matter. In my graveyard they buried Francis Jackson here. In Matt's graveyard they buried..." he looked across at the old man, waiting for a response.

"Frank Hamilton."

The boy nodded. "And for you the grave is John Deakin."

"I don't know why, but you're making it up to make fun of me."

The boy shook his head, a solemn motion that belonged to a man many times his age and it hit Sam like a train that the boy had been hanging around this graveyard for years or even decades. Long enough to age, even though he was still trapped inside the body of an eight-year-old boy.

"Why?" the boy asked. "Why go to all the trouble of pulling you out of your coffin just to make fun of you?" He stretched out his arms in a massive arc like a Snake Oil Salesman promising the world to a gullible punter. "This is your graveyard; it just isn't mine. Or Matt's. Or Betty's."

"So Paul?"

"Your brother? If he's dead, then he's over there. Like you said. Only you're never going to get to see him. Because no one crosses the wall. Not ever."

Sam looked at the kid.

"You're either one of them or one of us."

"Us?" Sam asked.

The boy rolled up his t-shirt. The side of his stomach was a churned-up mess of black and red muscle. Sam had seen enough cop shows to recognise a gunshot when he saw one.

"It was an accident. I didn't mean to do it, but apparently that don't make any difference over here."

"Over here?" Sam asked, but the idea was already lodged in his head and he put his hand to his throat to feel where the rope had burnt.

"You're one of us," the boy said. "Welcome to suicide alley."

CHAPTER EIGHT

Paul sat on the edge of a low tomb. Small stones pressed into the seat of his suit trousers. He and François had walked for miles, the rough earthly equivalent of five or more days, he estimated. It was hard to be sure here. He should be exhausted, but he wasn't. He should have tired feet, but they were fine. He should be thirsty or hungry, but his belly was sated.

So he sat, looking down at the round dell below him, and pretended to feel fatigue. The dell was one of nine around the base of the hill of souls, under the white glare of the chapel above. He could hardly see it now from his close vantage point. They called this dell the Roman Quarter. Paul supposed the Roman Ninth didn't have the same ring about it, but the laws of living physics and this plane made ugly bedfellows. A great arch, under two tall columns, kept the bleached skulls and bones from raining down on the shanty town market, which lay under its deep shadows. Paul wasn't sure what they had to sell or barter here; the fake hopes of the wretched dead were easily deceived.

He watched François laying on his charming French patter. If anyone could find a way to reach Sam, François would.

A stone tripped and bounced down the side of the sloping dell not more than twenty feet to his right. Paul looked around, half expecting to see someone standing at the top, but there was no one. He stared at the tombs and dark crevices to his right, but could see nothing. He turned his attention back to the market to see his friend coming out of a tent. Francois held the flap open and beckoned Paul towards him. Paul stood, brushed off the seat of his trousers, and carefully made his way down through the graveyard debris and rocks.

From the dark triangle of a broken tomb, something watched him walk across and enter the tent. The rear of the tomb had long been broken wide open, and a large-headed shadow exited and followed him down the slope.

The inside of the tent smelt sweaty and rank. A large brazier with yellow and blue flames sat in the centre of a stone table. Once a tomb lid, it had been turned over, covered with wire mesh and had burning coals underneath. A woman with a grey hood sat behind, half hidden by the smoke and heat haze.

"Paul, this is the lovely Urgunalla. She has agreed to help us on our odyssey." The Frenchman swept his arm towards the shrouded woman.

"Sit," the woman hissed.

Paul looked at François and raised his eyebrows. The Frenchman shrugged and raised his eyebrows in reply. They both moved together and sat on two of the stone seats before the exotic-smelling fire. The seats had no legs or backs and looked to Paul like they were sliced-up bits of fallen columns.

"Good," the woman said. Reaching down to unseen places, she produced bunches of dried herbs in each hand and threw them onto the centre of the wire-covered fire. They hissed and crackled and let off a luxurious smell that reminded both men of green meadows and hearty home-cooked meals.

"Tell me your names," she said, as she lowered her hood behind her mane of wild, black hair.

Paul winced at the sight of her face. Her left eye was open and appeared to have no eyelid, while the other was stained brown, sunken and sewn shut.

"Erm, I am François, and this is my friend Paul—"

"—No. Your names that belong to you here, that tell the tale of your ending." Her wide left orb flicked from one man to the next.

"I'm Paul the Passenger." It was a name he didn't use. It had been given to him by François, when he dug him up so many years ago.

François exhaled, puffing out his cheeks. He looked from the woman to Paul. "I'm Frankie the Fork," he finally said in a low voice.

"And whom do you seek?"

"My twin brother, Sam. He's just died."

"Give me your palms."

Paul looked at François and then at the flames. He gulped and held his arms over the smoky remains of the burnt herbs. His mind railed against this action and his eyes relayed the searing heat and flames up to his brain. But there was no heat or pain or suffering here. That was left behind on Earth. The woman lightly placed her hands on top of his.

"I am Urgunalla the Betrayed. My eye was lost. In the planes and realms beyond this one it seeks and it sees all things. Find now the twin brother of this man."

A puff of white smoke billowed up from the red coals below their joined hands. It hung, caught like a cloud above Paul's fingertips. Then it changed and a picture formed of a stone wall and a young boy standing by a grave. The vision showed smart-polished shoes and rose up to reveal a man that looked to Paul much like his dad. But it wasn't, it was his brother, Sam!

CHAPTER NINE

Sam turned and looked up to the sky, away from the boy's scarred stomach. He had a feeling that he was being watched. He stared up at the wall that cut a brutal line through the heart of the cemetery. There was nothing to explain the sensation that prickled the back of his neck and made his skin crawl. The summit of the wall was empty. The sky was a blank steel sheet, not even a bird wheeling against the backdrop.

"What is it?" the boy asked.

"Nothing," Sam said automatically. He looked back at the small group who had discovered him and tried to push away the feeling of being watched. It settled on him and even though it was impossible to ignore, he could at least resist the urge to seek it out. For now, at least.

The boy's damaged skin served as a reminder. "Suicide Alley?"

The boy shrugged. "You're one of us, aren't you?" There was a hunger to his words that made Sam uncomfortable. Without thinking, he brought his hand up to his throat and his fingers traced the grooves across his skin where the rope had cut into his neck.

"Let me guess, on the other side of the wall they're all having parties and hanging out with Jesus, but for our punishment we have to stay here in this desert. What, for eternity? No parole? No time off for good behaviour?"

The child twitched his head toward the wall and then looked back. It was a furtive movement, as if he was frightened of being seen.

"Shh," he said. "We don't talk about that."

"What?" Sam asked. He tried to determine what he had said that might have offended someone; he hadn't even done his old joke about the Jehovah's Witnesses. God, for a pack of dead people, this lot could be so touchy.

"We don't talk about them," the man said. He cast a glance over his shoulder, and it would have been comical except for the very real fear drawn across his face. Sam wondered if they were trying to wind him up, if it was some elaborate "play a joke on the newbie", but he dismissed the idea because he didn't think they were good enough actors. They were convincing because they were genuinely scared.

It was the woman who spoke. Her voice was low, almost a whisper. Sam wanted to point out that there was no one around to hear her, and yet as soon as she started to speak, the quiet tone of her voice felt appropriate.

"They come. The stink from their bones fills the air, and their screaming..." she shuddered, as if the memory was too real to bear. "Their screaming is the slaughter of innocents."

"Who are they?"

"I don't know." She said it slowly, the punch line to a joke that didn't make any sense to Sam. He felt the hairs on his arm stand up, as if a cold breeze had just blown across his skin. He turned around, unable to stop himself, and his mind filled with the creatures from the woman's description. He didn't know what he was seeing, and yet he was afraid of them. He hardly dared ask his next question.

"What do they want?"

"Souls," the woman said. A single word, drawn out long and thin. "Your essence. The only part of you that remains."

"We shouldn't even be talking to you," the boy said.

"They might come for us, too."

"We just wanted to protect you."

"We are taking a risk."

The small boy shuddered. "We are all taking a huge risk."

The man and the old crone looked at each other and nodded, as if confirming that what they were doing was so dangerous they were mad even to have considered it.

The boy turned quickly and peered into the distance. Sam

followed his gaze but couldn't see anything in the flat sky. The boy raised his hand to demand silence. He swayed slightly on the balls of his feet.

What's happening? What is it? Sam wanted to ask, but he was too afraid to speak. Too afraid that the creatures would rise up from the other side of the wall to seek him out.

"It's okay," the boy whispered. His words were barely audible, no louder than the shifting sands beneath their feet. "I thought I heard something, but I must have been mistaken."

"I thought I heard something too," the old woman said.

"Probably nothing," the man said. But he sounded like he didn't believe his own words and he raked his eyes along the horizon, as if he expected that *They* would come at any moment.

"We need to get you away from here," the boy said.

"Where?" Sam asked.

The boy thought for a moment. He dropped his head to one side. Sam could feel his heart pounding in his chest, and when he searched the landscape before him, his mouth was dry with fear. *Hurry up*, he wanted to urge him. The low graves all around offered no real protection. When they came, they would see him. And he was sure that when that moment arrived, his new friends would scatter and leave him to face the creatures alone.

"Please," Sam said. "You've got to help me."

The boy smiled, and just for an instant it was the smile of a predator.

"I've got an idea," he said. "I know where we can take you."

There was movement in the corner of the cemetery. The four of them turned their heads in perfect synchronisation. For the moment, it was a tiny speck of movement in the distance. A moment later, the voice reached them.

"Run," the boy said. He grabbed Sam's hand, and despite his small stature, he almost pulled Sam off his feet. "You need to come with us now."

CHAPTER TEN

Paul leaned forward and watched. Sam turned his head at the same time as the boy. They shouted at each other and began to run. Two other figures fled, too: a man and an old woman. Something dark swept past—dark, up close and hard to make out.

Urgunalla suddenly screamed and waved her hands through the orange mist until the vision melted away into spiralling wisps of smoke. The woman looked scared and her lidless eye hunted the upper confines of the tent.

"Hey, bring the picture back. That was my brother. Where is he? Who were those people?" Paul cried out, trying to get the attention of the woman's mad, roving eye.

"I cannot risk looking again. Dark things are abroad. If I had held the vision any longer, they might have crossed through to our world."

"What dark things?" François asked.

"Where is my brother?" Paul sat up in his stone chair. He wanted to grab the old woman and shake the answers out of her.

"Of those dark creatures I will never speak," she said, her one good eye on François. It then flicked to Paul. "His soul lies in Suicide Alley. That is the plane of the damned, where he will find neither rest nor enlightenment." The woman's shoulders sagged. She looked both unnerved and frail.

"Well, that's that then," François said as he stood and clapped his hands together. "Time to go, Paul. We gave it a good try, eh?" The Frenchman laid his hand lightly on his friend's shoulder as he moved to leave the smoky tent.

"What do you mean, that's it? He's still out there, we have to find him."

"You heard her, your brother killed himself. He is damned for eternity. We cannot help him now." Paul grasped his friend's arm but was easily shrugged off as François made for the tent flap.

Paul turned back to the woman and pleaded. "How can I get there? Show me the way."

"You will meet a tall, dark, handsome stranger," the woman said dryly in reply. "They will help you, if anyone can."

Paul licked his lips and stared down at Urgunalla, perplexed at what she had just said. He didn't know whether to laugh or cry.

"That was old even in my day, mon ami," François said as he left the tent.

Paul went to speak and then closed his mouth again. He ducked under the tent flap that his friend held and wondered what to do next.

A dark shadow crossed right in front of them. The two men gasped at the tall, dark-skinned, and pretty woman before them whose look screamed 1970s disco. Her height wasn't greater than Paul's, but her wild brown afro and the roller skates on her feet gave her a height advantage on most people. She wore a suede waistcoat with tassels over a pink too-tight t-shirt, exposing her belly button just above silver hotpants. Her ensemble was finished off by a pair of knee-high yellow-and-black-hooped socks.

"The name's Carmel Cunningham, but you can call me Cookie." She winked her extra-long fake eyelashes at the two men, eyeing them up in turn.

"Can we help you?" Paul managed to squeak out as his eye line was directly across from her impressive chest.

"Nope, brother, you can't," she replied in her American New York tones. "But I can help you two pale-looking fellas out."

François looked at Paul. Paul stared back at him, and then they slowly turned their confused faces back to the woman in front of them.

"How?" they both asked in unison, trying not to gulp afterwards.

"I hear you need a pilot. And I'm the most badass Boater-wrangling, plane-hopping *bitch* this side of hell, boys." Cookie grinned.

The two men could not help but smile back at her.

"You can do what for us?" Paul asked, not understanding ninety percent of what she had just said.

"You want passage to Suicide Alley and I'm the gal to take you," she said putting her hands on her hips. "You dig?"

"I have dug on occasions," François replied, wondering what that had to do with anything.

Now it was Cookie's turn to look confused. "So do you want my help or not?"

"If you can take us to Suicide Alley, then yes," Paul said.

"Then you better follow my fine ass outta here." Cookie spun on the spot and headed off inside the great arch under the hill of bones.

The two men looked at each other and shrugged. They followed Cookie into the tunnel beneath the great chapel.

"She does have a nice derrière," François whispered to his friend as they hurried to catch her.

"But can we trust her?" Paul whispered back. "And how do we pay her?"

She laughed from the darkness of a smaller side passageway ahead of them. "Cookie always finds ways for the men folk to pay."

The two men paused by the dark side tunnel, wary whether to proceed inside or not. A rushing noise came suddenly towards them, followed by a flash of flames. Cookie was before them again bending low in the smaller tunnel and holding a flaming torch in her left hand. Paul could now see that her nail varnish was bright purple.

"Are you boys ready for the ride of your lives?" she grinned.

CHAPTER ELEVEN

"Who are they? What do they want?" Sam asked, but when he got no response from any of the others, he stopped talking and tried to focus all his attention on running. Each step he took across the cemetery felt like his legs were cloaked in mud. Within a minute, his mad run had slowed to a stagger.

"Wait!" he called to the others. They were already far in front and moving fast. They dodged between the gravestones with a grace that seemed impossible. Sam looked behind him. And stopped.

He had moved no more than thirty foot from his own grave. He saw the mound of dirt to one side of his wooden grave marker. He felt a physical ache at the sight. The pain came so sudden and hard that he dropped to his knees and clutched his chest. *I'm having a heart attack,* he thought, *only twenty-eight and I'm having a fucking heart attack.*

He tried to call out but there was no air in his lungs with which to make a sound. In his head the noise of his chest was a death rattle, and in that instant, he found a memory of the moment he stepped off the chair. Until then he had not known he was going to go through with it. He'd thought about it. He'd thought about it every day since he'd woken up in the hospital with his father sitting beside his bed waiting to tell him that Paul was dead and it was all his fault, but until he had stepped off the chair and felt the rope tighten against his throat, he had never quite believed he had the guts to actually do it.

"But I did," he whispered to himself. The words came out as a strangled noise, impossible to understand.

And now he was going to die for a second time. He didn't

know how it was possible, and yet the agony in his chest convinced him that there was no other explanation. Someone had cracked open his ribs and stuck a handful of burning straw into his chest.

The world went black and the loudest sound was his own ragged breathing. He had time to wonder what would happen next—would he awake in another coffin, buried this time in a cemetery for loser-suicides who couldn't even do that properly—and then light flooded into his eyes as if someone had shone a torch into his face.

At first, the white light burnt out any detail. He blinked, not sure if it would make a difference, but gradually he began to make out shapes. Still no detail, just grey shapes.

The sound of his own breathing faded into the background. He heard voices that grew louder as the shapes became more distinct. There was something familiar about the voices … he stretched to grab hold, but it was just beyond his understanding.

"We gotta leave him."

Sam snatched at the sound like a child playing with toy bricks. There was something there, something he couldn't understand if he tried hard enough.

"We gotta leave."

"He must be still attached. I told you to break the cord."

"Who died and made you God?"

"Well do something now or we're going to lose him."

"Cut the cord. I'm not going to lose this one, too."

The pain in Sam's chest intensified until it felt that someone had fired up a blast furnace in there. He tried to breathe, but it was impossible. He felt tears run from his eyes and down his cheeks, and he was powerless to do anything. What would Paul think if he saw him now? He'd probably punch him in the shoulder hard enough to deaden the muscle and then call him a wuss. But maybe Paul would understand. After all, he must have been through this as well.

I'm going to die, Sam thought.

It was impossible, inconceivable, and yet the pain intensified. Now he didn't worry that he was going to die, he was more afraid that he would not. These were the fires of hell that the vicar had warned him about from the pulpit on the few times he had been dragged into church. This was the agony reserved especially for him by God or the devil. Killer of brother, killer of self.

Someone screamed. The noise cut through the pain. A scream and then the pain stopped. It didn't fade, it simply stopped.

Images rushed in to assault him: the faces of the three of them peering at him. For a moment he was back in the coffin after they had just pulled him out of the ground.

"What happened?" Sam wasn't sure he could speak, but his words came out. They were a little breathless, a little fractured, but proper words all the same.

"Dumbo here forgot to cut your cord," the child said.

For all his size, the man managed to look like a scolded boy sent to the corner of the room to do penance. "Sorry."

"Cord?"

"Your umbilicus," the old woman said. "If you don't cut the cord, then it's impossible to move beyond your resting place. Isn't it, Matt?" As she said the last phrase, she glared at the man and he nodded with dumb acceptance.

"I thought I was dying."

The child nodded. "Yeah, I know the feeling. But we ain't got time to talk about that now. We've got to move. Those lot are getting closer."

Sam looked to the corner of the graveyard. It was still there, a mass of churning motion.

The child grabbed him by the arm. "We gotta go now. Before they catch us. Before they catch you."

"Catch me? They're hardly moving."

Sam looked from the black, churning mass on the horizon to the high wall. "Paul's over there?"

"You can't get to him," the child said. "Can't you get that into your thick skull? We can't cross over there and they can't come over here."

"Why?"

"Why?" The boy turned to the other two. "Why, he asks!" He turned back to Sam. "Because that's how it works. I don't make the rules, none of us do."

"I've never been a good one for rules," Sam said. "Ask Paul."

The wall was a simple, flat structure with no distinguishing features. Sam picked a spot at random, away from the mob that churned at the edge of the cemetery, and then started to walk in that direction.

"Where are you going?"

Sam didn't bother to slow. They would just use any hesitation as another opportunity to try and convince him to go with them.

"To find my brother," he told them. "To find Paul and say sorry."

He chose not to turn around, but after only a few paces he heard the three behind him wrapped in an argument, and then a moment later their footsteps rattled on the gravel as they hurried to catch up with him. Paul was right, he did always get his own way.

CHAPTER TWELVE

"So how did the big ol' Reaper come claim you boys?" Cookie's voice was strong and echoed loudly around the cavernous darkness.

The two men next to her on the ledge jumped a little after what had seemed to Paul like hours of dark silence. The torches had fluttered away to embers ages ago and any conversation with them. There was a cold updraft coming from the ebony vast abyss only inches from where they sat. Paul sat with his knees drawn up to his chest. His spine was pressed against the cavern wall and his arms hugged his legs. He didn't feel the cold anymore, but this place was the closest experience he had to it since he had passed away.

"Okaaaay," Cookie purred. "Cat got your tongues? Well let me start the skates rolling. In ninety-seventy-six I was kicking back in a friend's basement listening to Marvin Gaye. I was sitting on his father's old swivel chair, legs up on an old desk. My friend Delvine went to fetch some booze and I was in a peckish mood, if you know what I mean. There was a plate of homemade cookies her momma had baked up for us. So I began to wolf one down, started choking, a big ol' lump stuck in my windpipe. Couldn't get up, fell off the chair and that, my friends, was the end of Carmel Cunningham. Shit way for such a sexy sassy lady like me to go."

"What is a Cookie?" François asked.

"Large biscuit, mate," Paul replied. "So you died choking on a cookie?"

"No point being embarrassed about it, this is the plane of accidental deaths. You either embrace that or be a timid … dead … fuck."

"Good point." Paul nodded in the darkness. "Mine was a car accident. My brother was driving, we were coming back from a party. Both of us far too pissed to drive, but the bravery of youth made us think we were indestructible. We were twins, did everything together, the *terrible two* against the world. It was dark. I bent down to change the CD. Sam swore. I looked up and saw bright lights in my eyes. Something large hit us. Then *wham,* blackness and here. End of story."

"Your brother survived the crash?"

"Yes, but Sam has just killed himself and I've got to find him. Mostly I want to hug him and forgive him. The anger soon dies or it will turn you mad."

"Ain't that the truth," Cookie replied, shifting slightly in the darkness. "What about you *Frenchie,* how did you meet your maker?"

"Oh, you'll be lucky, it took me a year to get that information out of him," Paul chuckled.

"Ain't scared, are you, Frenchie?" Cookie chided.

"François Thomas is not scared of anything. I just won't share my personal life with a complete stranger, that's all." Paul could almost taste the moodiness coming from the Frenchman's lips.

"Pitchfork to the back of the neck," Paul blurted out.

"Merde," François swore. "Is nothing sacred to you … you little English wanker!"

"Hey, remember Agincourt, you old tosser. Secret's out now, so tell the nice lady the full story, mate."

François swore again and let out a sulky exhale. "My sister was in the upper barn and threw the pitchfork at a pile of hay. She missed and impaled me through the neck. One moment I was standing there, the next I had a spike of metal erupting through my Adam's apple. Not the best way for a brave Frenchman to die. There, see. You have my story now, mock all you want."

Paul heard François refold his arms in anger and the place grew silent again. Cookie's loud voice finally pierced the void.

"Mother-fucker!"

"Is that insult aimed at me?" François gruffly asked.

"Not everything is about you, Frenchie," Cookie said. "Looky here boys, here comes our ride."

Paul was about to say *where,* but stopped as he caught sight of what Cookie had spotted. Something was moving in the abyss ten feet or so below the thin ledge on which they sat. It was mainly black, like the darkness, but gave out a purple glow from its vast underbelly. It was hard to comprehend its huge bulk, or where it began or ended. He could make out slimy black legs and a smudged smoke-like oiliness that followed it. It stunk of a thousand nappy sacks rotting in a vegetable compost heat. The stench made Paul feel lightheaded.

Where the end of its long feeler-like legs touched the darkness, they illuminated a purple film, like it was an insect walking on Clingfilm.

"What do we do?" Paul asked, trying not to breathe through his nostrils.

"We take the next Greyhound out of here *motherfuckers,*" Cookie cried with obvious delight.

"You have to be fucking joking, woman. We cannot ride that monstrosity," François shouted back. The cavernous black hole was filled with a scuttling sound.

"Not scared are you, Frenchie?" Cookie baited. She leapt over the side, down onto the undulating back of the creature.

"My name is François, you stupid whore," he swore, and with snarling lips followed her over the ledge.

"Fuck it," Paul said, standing on the edge of the ledge. "Sam, the things I do for you."

Paul leapt into the abyss, wailing his head off.

CHAPTER THIRTEEN

They followed Sam for half an hour. He couldn't see them but he heard their constant bickering behind him. There were times he wanted to turn around and bellow at them to shut up, but he was still not convinced the whole thing was not an act. He couldn't think of any reason why they would conspire to keep him from the wall, but the feeling remained and over the years he had learned to trust his instincts. It was when he ignored them he usually got into trouble, like snatching the car keys and thinking he was perfectly able to drive home when he couldn't even walk in a straight line.

The wall was getting closer and despite what he had said to the kid, he wasn't eager to reach it. From the other side of the cemetery, it had looked no higher than a garden fence, but then he never had been much good at perspective—his art teacher had made a point of telling him every time he submitted a piece of work. At last, he was beginning to accept she might have been telling the truth. The kid was right—there was no way he was going to be able to climb that. It had to be at least eighty feet tall.

He let the other three catch up with him. The kid walked beside him, his head drooped down and his hands clasped together behind his back like an old man. The other two hung back a step.

"You really mean to do this?" the boy asked.

"Yes." Sam didn't look at the wall when he spoke.

"You think you'll find your brother over there? Drinking wine and eating peeled grapes?"

"Something like that." In truth, Sam hadn't thought what it would be like for Paul. The two of them had been apart for too long, that was the only thing that was important. Even if Paul was burning in the fiery pit of Hades, he needed to be with him. Although, now that he was finally thinking about it, if this dry, desolate graveyard was all the afterlife had to punish him for all he had done, then Paul, who had lucked out with the stupid twin brother he'd been attached to from birth, deserved better. Surely that was the point of the wall—Sam didn't deserve whatever was on the other side.

"It isn't going to be like that," the boy said.

"You been over there?" Sam asked.

The boy shook his head. "Don't you listen? You can't get across."

"Why not?"

"Because we're the damned. You. Me. Those two. This is our punishment. Maybe it's different in some of the other places, but there ain't no point getting worked up about them because you're never going to see them. The wall is there to remind us of that."

"But people do cross?"

"Why the hell would anyone want to come here? Look at this place!" He swiped his arm in a grand gesture that managed to take in the sweeping plane of the cemetery and the huddle of the slowly moving mob in the distance. "You can't rest, because if you stop moving for too long they'll catch up with you. There's nothing to eat. Nothing to drink. This is hell right here. It might not seem it to you yet, but in time it will."

"But people cross?" Sam pressed.

"Forget it. You're just going to drive yourself mad. Everything is in the hands of the Great Creator. Give yourself up to him and you will find peace. Not joy, because you don't deserve joy, but peace. The Great Creator creates, and there is the other one you do not want to find, the Great Cremator. They sound much the same, but the Cremator only wants your soul to burn."

Great, a religious nut, Sam thought to himself. *I had enough run-ins with them before.* When he came out of prison after the accident, he thought he'd be allowed to wallow in self-pity, but instead *they* had found him. *They* had wanted to save him from himself, to help him to repent and find his way to the Good

Lord. It was strange, and the only thing he really noticed about them was the way that when they spoke, their words seemed to be in capitals. It didn't matter what it was, whether it was that He Needed To Make His Peace With The Lord or Did He Want Fries With That? It had taken months of hiding away before the God botherers had finally given up on him and found a new soul to save. Strange, he would not have spotted the kid and his two cronies for the God Squad.

"So the Great Creator, is he the boss around here? Could he get me over the wall?"

"He could," the kid said slowly. There was something about the drawn-out phrase that gave Sam the creeps. Something subtly off-kilter about the way he spoke, as if behind those two words was hidden a ream of small print.

"Do you want us to take you to him?" the old woman asked. She was eager, too eager for Sam.

"No. I'm fine for now. Thanks."

"He can help," the man said from behind him. His voice was slippery, like blood on ice.

"I'll bear that in mind."

The kid was silent. Sam almost wished he would pile in too so he could get all the refusals out of the way at the same time. Instead, the kid simply followed in silence with his hands clasped behind his back.

They walked, winding between gravestones, getting closer and closer to the wall that scraped the steel-blue sky. Sam focussed his eyes on the base of the wall. He inspected the orange stone. As the detail of the structure was revealed to him, he noticed the uneven surface of the stones, as if they had been hewn from a rock face with awkward hands and few tools. They were arranged in a jagged pattern, like bricks in a wall. There was no sign of mortar between them, as if the sheer weight of the wall was the only thing that held the structure in place.

He stopped. Turned and looked back over the cemetery. He tried to make out the spot where his grave had been, but it was impossible to see.

Behind him the wall loomed above his shoulders. He looked at the ground in front of him and noticed that it did not cast a shadow, that none of them cast a shadow. Sam looked up into the sky and realised that although it was light, there was no sign of the sun. And the light … it hadn't changed at all since he had been broken out of his coffin. He wasn't sure exactly how long ago that was, but it had to have been hours; it felt like he had been walking toward the wall for days.

He opened his mouth to make his observation to the other three, but decided against it. Either they already knew or they didn't care enough to notice.

The wall was behind him. He had assumed just reaching the wall was an achievement, but now that he was here, he realised the kid was right. It towered above him. Beneath it he felt no more significant than a tick on a bedsheet.

He brushed his hand against the rough surface of the rock. He was sweating with the heat. Tired and hungry and thirsty. All this was still new to him. But Paul was on the other side. Paul was somewhere over there and he had to find him, even if it meant taking the wall down stone by stone.

Sam laughed to himself.

"What's so funny?"

"Stone by stone," Sam said. "After all, I've got all the time in the world. I've got eternity."

He pressed the palm of his hand against the wall, and the scream buried itself in him.

CHAPTER FOURTEEN

Even though it wasn't possible anymore, Paul felt sick to his stomach. He, like his companions, stood waist deep in some purple gelatinous goo that stunk worse than bottled and fermented hundred-day-old cat piss.

Paul had heard the term *inside the belly of the beast*, but never thought he'd get so close to realising it. Cookie, François, and he were lined up in a row, taking up three of the five holes in the rear abdomen of the enormous creature. He was near the rear back left leg, covered by layers of chitinous armour plating. The constant lurching movements of the beast and the semen-like sacks of purple bodily fluid they stood in made for the queasiest rides ever.

Even Cookie's motor-mouth stopped prattling on after the first hour. François held one hand over his mouth and gulped in short draughts of the foetid air as quickly as possible. They travelled on the outer edges of the planes of death in near darkness. Only the purple glow of the liquid in which they travelled shone any light onto their nightmare journey. Paul remembered being stuck with Sam on a trip to London once, in a broken-down tube carriage in the middle of summer. It felt as wretched as that, but they had only endured that for thirty minutes or so. This felt like forever.

"Okay, people, time to jump ship," Cookie yelled with both her hands cupped around her mouth.

"Jump where?" François asked, removing his hand from his mouth for a moment.

"Out into the bright blue yonder, gentlemen. So pull up your socks and grab your cocks, it's bailout time." Paul watched amazed as Cookie pulled herself out of her gooey hole and stood up riding the side of the Boater, with roller skates on her feet.

"I can't see anything," Paul said, pulling one foot out of the slurping mess and onto the side of the hole in the Boater's lower armour.

"Best that way, hun," she replied with a wink. "Help me with your friend here."

It took all their strength to pull the unwilling Frenchman from his purple pouch of slime. They held hands and carefully moved down the armoured body to the gap between it and the back leg. They peered over the side. The view wasn't very helpful. The Boater's three-jointed leg touched the skin of another world. It was like they were balanced on the side of a soap bubble. Nothing could be seen below but the purple illuminated skin of some other world.

"So is this the place where my brother is?"

"No," Cookie replied.

"No?" Paul and François said together.

"No." She nodded. "This gets us nearer to him, but there is no direct route to the Plane of Suicides. *He* forbids it. But we are closer than before and have a long journey ahead. So if you girls are ready, we'll jump on my count of three."

"Wait, wait, hold on a minute. You never told us about this before?" François looked even paler than normal.

"Well, you never really asked, did you, Frenchie?" Cookie put her free hand on her hip and raised her eyebrows at the two men.

"Please refrain from calling me that."

Cookie turned away from François. "Okay, Pauline, you seem a little less dense than your honky brother here. This ain't no daytrip outta Harlem to Coney Island. We are doing some serious fucked-up-against-the-rules shit here. We can't just parachute our sexy asses down into the place where your brother is. It will take stealth, courage, and Cookie Cunningham to guide you there by roads unseen, darlings. This route is full of danger and it's already too late for you to turn back. So we either motherfucking jump in the next ten seconds or we'll miss our stop."

François looked from Cookie to Paul.

"But we *are* getting one step closer to Sam though?" Paul asked to delay the jump into the void below.

"In a roundabout way, yes," she replied, looking down past her roller skates to the darkness they were about to plummet into.

"What does that mean?" Paul flapped his right hand against his side in frustration.

"It means we have to go kinda out and around to get to the correct stop. Thangs aren't just left, right and up, down around here. You dig?"

"Not really." Paul shook his head. The realisation that this was the worst idea a dead man ever had was finally dawning on him.

"Look, I used to have the same run-around conversations with my man back in the day. You know what I used to say then, boys?"

"No, what?" Paul replied.

"Go jump." Cookie leapt off the side of the Boater as she shouted. François, who was holding her right hand, screamed as he was pulled after her. Paul hardly had time to cry out as he was yanked forwards by François's right hand and pitched over the side of the Boater.

The three companions hit the film of the plane below and passed right through. It felt like begin caught in a thundery shower for a second. Yet they emerged through the film of a different world as dry as ever. The ground was close and hurtling up to meet their scared faces. The new world below was cast in an eye-piercingly white glow, as their dark speck-like bodies plummeted into the ground at supersonic speed.

CHAPTER FIFTEEN

Sam pulled his hand away from the wall and looked down at his palm. He wasn't sure what he expected to find—maybe a red weal or a burn—but his skin was flawless. He stroked his hand, but the touch of his ragged fingers upon his skin summoned no feeling, no feeling at all.

Behind him the woman laughed. Her low *huck-huck-huck* was more irritating than Sam could have believed possible and he was filled with the urge to turn around and punch her to shut her up. But he didn't hit women—that was one of the rules. One of the things that Paul and he had always agreed on, even in the darkest days when it felt like their lives were going to hell, was they didn't hit women and they didn't hurt children. Everyone else was fair game.

"Shut up," Sam said. His words only encouraged her to laugh more loudly.

"You found the wall, dintcha? Just like you wanted. So what you gonna do now?"

Tear it down, one stone at a time, Sam thought. He almost laughed himself, at his pig-headed stupidity which had suggested that he could do anything against the wall. Maybe hanging himself had killed a few of his brain cells along the way. Paul had always said that they were in short supply, but then Paul had drunk that shot glass of petrol as a bet, so he had no room to talk.

He put his hand out to touch the wall and again the scream rose up. It came from inside him. As if the noise had its origins in his stomach and his liver and his bones. The sound had a strangled, drawn-out quality as if it were one note stretched to eternity. There was no possibility that it would ever stop. When he took his hand away for the second time, the scream continued to live in his jaw and his teeth, rattling around inside his head.

"What is it?" Sam asked.

The child answered with a shrug. "Something to keep you here."

Sam looked up. From his spot it looked like the wall had no limit, as if it might stretch up into the sky until it pushed through the clouds and just keep on going. But he had seen the top, he knew that all he had to do was keep climbing and eventually he would master the wall.

He gritted his teeth, placed one hand on the wall and found a fingerhold between the stones and pulled himself off the ground. Just a couple of inches, hardly a miracle, and yet against the background of the incessant screaming it felt like the greatest achievement ever made.

"You really gonna climb the wall?" the old woman asked.

Sam didn't answer; it took all his effort to stay on the wall. His face was so close to the stone it brushed the tip of his nose. He could taste the dry stone at the back of his throat. His fingers clung tightly to the edge of the stone. He lifted his leg and scrabbled his toes against the stones to feel out a hold, and once he had one, he pushed against it and lifted his body another precious few inches closer to the top of the wall.

"He can't do it," the old woman said.

"Maybe."

"No. It isn't possible." The child's voice cut through the other two.

"How do you know? Have you tried?"

"The wall is inviolable."

"But you never tried it?"

Sam tried to brush away the sounds of the voices. There was nothing to be gained by listening to their bickering. He had to concentrate on staying on the wall, on inching up and up until he reached the top. He tried to push out of his mind what would happen if he fell down. Was it possible to die again? The image of his body lying cracked on the dry ground at the base of the wall was as strong as a memory.

He reached his hand up. He had his eye on a crack in a stone just to the left of his head. The screaming rinsed through his body. It churned up a nausea that made him want to curl into a ball.

"Maybe it's a way out."

"No," the child said.

Maybe it was just Sam's imagination, and maybe it was just hopeful thinking, but he thought he detected a note of doubt in that flat denial. Perhaps the kid didn't know as much as he thought. Maybe it just took a bit more imagination, a bit more guts. Paul had always told him he had enough guts to lead an army into battle—guts or stupidity, sometimes it was difficult to separate them.

Sam snatched for another hold and for a second his fingers closed on nothing but air. He felt the sickening lurch of his body as his full weight fell onto the tiny ledge on the wall where his toes were jammed. He slapped his hand against the wall, fingertips scratching at the rock. One fingernail bent back and there was a moment of perfect black pain that eclipsed everything.

He pushed the pain out of his mind and concentrated on hanging on to the wall. He pressed his cheek against the rough stones. His harsh breathing echoed inside his head. *Come on, come on,* he urged himself. *You can do this.*

Slowly the sense of falling faded. The muscles in his arms shook at the effort of holding on. He wanted to look up and see how close he was to the top, or look down and see how far he had managed to travel, but he didn't dare, and instead he stared at the carved stone inches away from his eyes.

A trickle of sweat ran down his forehead and into his eyes. Stinging salt blurred his vision and he tried to blink it away.

"The Great Creator would not allow it."

"Maybe he doesn't know."

"Maybe he doesn't care."

There was a stunned silence at the sacrilege. Even Sam could hear it.

"The Great Creator knows everything," the child intoned. "He sees all."

"But climbing the wall," the woman said. "Did it ever occur to you to try?"

"There is no escape from the garden of lost souls," the child said. "There is only the Great Creator."

"But..."

"There is no escape," the child repeated. Sam felt as if the boy was no longer responding to the woman but rather repeating his litany for the benefit of the idiot trying to climb the wall.

No escape? Sam thought. *I'll show them.* He was just too chicken to try.

The screams had almost faded to a dull ache now. They were there, always there, and yet not as strong as they had been, or maybe he was getting used to them. He reached up with his fingers and found a handhold above his head and dragged his body up another few feet. He grinned. *Wait until I tell Paul about this.*

The stone crumbled beneath his fingers. A chunk of the wall fell away. Sam reached out a hand but instinctively he knew it was impossible. He was off-balance. Wind rushed against his face. He grabbed a fistful of air and then he was falling backwards.

He landed on the ground. The impact pushed the air from his lungs.

The other three surrounded him, staring down at him as he lay in the dirt.

"Five feet," the child said. "He only climbed five feet. I told you it couldn't be done."

Sam hauled himself to his feet. He looked back at the wall. There was a crack in the rock, just a few feet above his head. A crack that looked like a small piece of the stone had only very recently been dislodged to expose the pristine white surface below. The child was right. Just a few feet off the ground.

He put his hand against the wall and the screaming started up once more. And he began to climb.

CHAPTER SIXTEEN

"*Holyshittingfuckinghell*—what is that?" Paul screeched, his voice almost reaching Bee-Gees falsetto heights as he ran.

François's only reply was a continuous scared warbling, "*Nerrrrrrh*" sound, as he picked up his longer legs and sprinted ahead of his friend. Paul could see a line of trees ahead, dusted with snow that covered the whole area about a foot deep. François was making a beeline for the large copse. Paul angled his escape run after the fleeing dead Frenchman. He forced the tight muscles in his neck to turn his head and see how Cookie was doing.

She was the most inadequately dressed of the trio. Her roller skates were heavy, cumbersome, and slowing her down. As François was almost ten feet ahead of Paul now, so Cookie was about the same distance or more behind him. She had the longest legs of them all, but the giant inhuman monstrosity following them was bearing down on her.

It was some pale giant horror from a realm of imagination Paul could not fathom. It was white like the surrounding snow and had two legs the height and width of large beech trees. There anything remotely connected with a living Earth flora or fauna ended. It had a vast white trunk, but no head or visible features. Long sinewy arms or branches protruded from its body like a huge loping brush. The appendages went out and then bent downwards, searching for the invaders. At the end of each appendage were twenty or more pink, wiggling, boneless digits. They rippled in the snow-dotted breeze that flew sidewards into the fleeing trio.

"Keep running," Cookie yelled, urging Paul on towards the snow-covered trees.

He turned back in time to see François run into what they hoped was the safety of the trees. He could see nothing in the wilderness to use as a weapon, so he pumped his arms and followed François. He ran into the woods. The trees were stubby with a low canopy just above his head. He hoped this would make it difficult for the sixty-foot giant white thing to come in after them.

François had stopped about thirty feet inside the small wood. The Frenchman was leaning forwards with his hands on his knees, panting hard. Paul halted beside him. He was glad that he didn't have to feel the burning pain in his lungs anymore. He leant against the ice-covered tree trunk next to him, as Cookie finally make it under the cover of the trees.

The white, gangling, many-armed giant had stopped dead in its considerable tracks. Puffing her cheeks out, Cookie joined the two men, with many looks back at the stationary creature outside.

"Either it can't see very well, or it doesn't want to come in after us." Cookie leant on Paul's shoulder as she shook out her long legs.

"What in the seven hells was that thing?" François asked, keeping his eyes on the thick white legs of the monstrous giant thing outside. "And where—the fuck—are we?"

"That's nothing I've ever seen before, even in some whacked-out horror film." Paul waved towards the beast.

Cookie stepped back from his wild arms and moved three steps to lean against her own tree. "Dunno, man. Never seen anything like him here before. Musta been lucky on my other trips. Bit of a rush eh … *my boys*."

"A rush?" François sneered. "Well, we certainly had to *rush* to get away from it. Please tell me things like that were not around when both of you were alive."

"Things like that, you've got to be joshing, mate. That's something out of someone's worst nightmare." Paul realised he was over-gesticulating, as he did sometimes, and crossed his arms to stop himself.

"That thing is not from Earth, you dopes. You two just don't get the bigger picture, do you?" Cookie stood looking at them both, her hands on her hips.

"What do you mean, madam?" François asked, peering around the large-haired woman to make sure the giant white monster was still outside the copse.

"This and the place we came from is like a great mess of planes connected to one another, like wool bundled up in a ball. Imagine each quarter of an inch is a different plane of afterlife. Billions upon trillions of different heavens, hells, and in-betweens wrapped up together. Now these strings touch other strings of wool in the ball. On the edges of the strings the Boaters scramble about. So we can move our asses from one plane to the other, until we pass through enough of the right places to find Paul's brother. You get it now, *hunny-childs*?"

François's and Paul's silence made Cookie frown, shake her head, and run her long fingernails through her afro. "Look, Earth is just one iddy-biddy world in a greater universe. Other planets and other life forms, *Jim*, but not as we know it. Each of those planets with differing life on them, they too have their own afterlives and planes where the dead go. The ball I had you imagine is infinite in size. Man, just thinking about it blows my mind."

Paul looked at Cookie with growing respect. He gazed past her towards the thick white legs of the creature beyond. An alien creature, from a distant alien world, but also dead like they were. Paul wondered if this snowy wasteland was its idea of heaven or hell. Maybe this was where its kind yearned to go after death. The escalating thoughts in his mind threatened to explode his dead brain. He could not express what he was feeling, so he just looked at Cookie, nodded and smiled.

She returned his smile warmly.

"Fascinating as that is, what do we do now?" François spoke, breaking the spell between Paul and Cookie.

Just then the giant beast began ripping up the trees in the copse three or four at a time.

"We run," Cookie cried, and was away on her snow-hindered wheels. The two men turned and ran after her.

CHAPTER SEVENTEEN

Sam lay on his back and stared up into the sky. He could hear his three companions muttering to each other just out of sight. They did that a lot; a guy could get a complex about all those whispered conversations.

He tried to ignore them. They couldn't help him. They were too locked in their own understanding of this hell and they weren't able to think beyond it. Their heads were stuck in a litany of can't: can't climb the wall, can't walk around the wall, can't escape. If it was up to those three, he would spend the rest of his eternity trapped in this place. With no chance of ever meeting Paul again.

"I made a mistake," he called over to them. "Is that such a terrible thing that I should be damned for eternity?"

Either they didn't hear him or they chose not to answer.

From his position the wall looked impossibly tall, and so it had proved. Ten times he had tried to climb up the side of the structure, but in the end, after ten falls when he had never reached more than a fraction of the distance to the top, he had to accept that maybe the boy was right—climbing the wall was no way to escape.

His fingers ached from his efforts to find handholds in the raw stone. He'd lost another fingernail on his last attempt and his knees were rubbed raw from pressing against the wall. Part of him wanted to lie down, stare up at the motionless sky, and forget about everything.

But he couldn't—because even something as simple as that reminded him of Paul, and being reminded of Paul rekindled the urge, no, the absolute *need*, to find his brother. Maybe if he'd been a praying man, he would have been able to make peace with his brother before now—offer up a torrent of words in a smoky church somewhere: three Our Fathers, ten Hail Marys, and a good act of contrition. But if he'd been that way inclined, he probably wouldn't have been belting down the back roads with more alcohol than blood in his veins in the first place, and he would definitely not have stepped off a chair with a noose strapped around his neck.

As he lay there feeling the hard earth press into his spine and stones burrow their way into his skin, he remembered lying in a field with Paul, the pair of them looking up into the sky. They were drunk; it seemed to Sam that in those last few months together they had always been drunk.

Sam reached out his hand, the memory of that night so close that he felt he could stretch out and wrap his fingers around the bottle of Becks' planted between them. When he closed his hand around nothing but dry air, he felt a pang of loss ring through him.

If he remembered correctly, it was Paul who said it. Paul who had laid down in the long grass and suggested that they look up into the night sky and watch the world spinning. Sam recalled he had made some crass joke that the reason everything was spinning had less to do with the motion of the earth and everything to do with the 5.1% absolute volume of the beer.

"Do you ever wonder what it's all about?" Paul had asked when they were both lying on the wet grass. Sam wasn't paying attention; he was more interested in the fact that his clothes were getting wet. He looked up into the sky, past cotton-wool clouds. Stars glittered like chips of diamonds.

"I know what it's all about. It's about girls and booze."

As soon as he said it, he felt stupid. As if he had ruined something special.

But Paul chose to ignore him, and Sam felt that warm glow of gratitude that just reminded him that they might be twins, and yet somehow when they were still in their mother's womb, they had been made different. Paul had been given the smarts. He didn't just mean intelligence—they were both clever enough to get away with stuff when they put their minds to it.

No, what Paul had was something different, something deeper. He had the ability to know when to shut up and just stare into space, and when to ignore his twin brother if he made a stupid remark. It had been Paul who had found the back route into the cemetery that time with Trish and Joanne, and Paul couldn't be held responsible for the fact those two girls had freaked at the idea of making out amongst the gravestones.

"Do you ever wonder whether there are other planets out there with people just like us? Maybe somewhere else right now there are a couple of eighteen-year-old kids staring into space, looking right back at us."

Sam held his tongue, not trusting himself to say anything.

"It's probably crap," Paul said, "but I like to think about it anyway. It beats the alternative which is that this is all a fluke, a one-off. That we hang around for a few years, waste our lives in dead-end jobs, have a couple of squalling kids, then we croak it and they dump us in a hole in the ground and ten million Chinamen don't give a shit. Am I right?"

"Amen," Sam said.

Sam opened his eyes and stared up into the sky. "Amen," he muttered to himself, and then imagined Paul rolling his eyes and making some smart-aleck remark about how he'd got religion and that would be the death of him.

What would Paul do? he thought to himself. He wouldn't give up. That's what he would do.

Sam grinned to himself. And then felt like hitting himself on the head.

"Stupid," he said. He heard a sound from beyond his vision and imagined the three companions were coming closer to see why their latest addition was talking to himself. "Sometimes you are the most stupid man in four countries, Samuel Wright. If Paul is here, then he's going to be looking for you, too."

Sam sat up. Too quickly. He had to wait for the dizzy spell to pass. His three companions were stationed just a little distance from him, crowded in a huddle but looking his way as if they had been caught in the middle of gossiping about him.

"My brother will be looking for me! Don't you get it? I don't have to climb the wall. I don't have to get out. He'll come for me. Paul will find me, I know it."

The three of them stared at Sam. That moment of enlightenment stubbornly refused to trouble their expressions, but he wrote it off as petulance. They didn't like the fact that he had worked it out. Or that they didn't have someone in their lives like Paul—someone who would do anything and go anywhere to find him.

The boy stepped forward. To Sam it looked like he was struggling not to smile.

"Your brother is not coming for you. He won't even know that you're dead." And then he did smile, Sam was sure of it. It was all Sam could do to stop himself from curling his hand into a tight fist and knocking that bastard over on his heels.

"No," Sam said, "that isn't true. Paul will know." But as he said it, he heard the truth of the boy's words. Paul had been here for thirteen years already. Why would he expect his twin brother to have followed after him so quickly?

"I'm not giving up," Sam said. He turned his back on the boy, on all three of them. "I'm not giving up," he muttered to himself and began scouring the face of the wall for a handhold to begin his next attempt.

CHAPTER EIGHTEEN

Paul ran out the other side of the woods, soon catching up with Cookie. François was still in front of him. Lucky for them, the copse held up the giant creature. It could not slide between the trees, but instead had to bash them aside or pull them up, roots and all.

"Down the valley to the left," Cookie cried out. Paul saw François swerve in that direction through the thinning snow. He ran after him. It led to a long dell, bordered by a rocky outcropping on either side.

"Left-left," Cookie shouted from behind.

Paul ran in that direction; he had little choice unless he wanted to scale the high sides of the valley they were running through. It triggered a memory of a hill from his childhood. In the winter, if it snowed enough, it made a scary toboggan run. Even in summer he and Sam dared each other to run down it at full pelt and that was nerve-wracking enough. Paul lost count of the times Sam or he had tripped over a stone or gnarled root and gone flying. They used to come home with the knees of their jeans ripped. Most times they would get sent to bed, whatever the hour, with their ears ringing and no dinner. Their mum would do all the shouting, while dad would tut and vow to take the money for new jeans out of their savings accounts. He never did though and would often sneak them up some leftovers when their mother was watching her soaps.

In their shared bedroom they would count up the scratches and nettle stings to see who had been the toughest that day. Outside, the chiming of an ice-cream van or the torturous sounds of kids still playing on the green would make their punishment worse. They were usually punished as a pair, which made their bedroom prison a little better. Only a couple of times did Paul get sent on a trip up the *wooden hill to Bedfordshire* alone. Usually when he'd done something awful to his twin, but that wasn't often.

The roaring sound of the monster shook him out of his remembrances. He looked behind to see Cookie catching up to him. The snow was nearly gone and what looked like the cracked remains of a road twisted round and down. As they made their flight along the road, the air seemed warmer than before, like some Saharan breeze coming up the slope. Parts of a broken fence lay on the right side of the road. It was shaped like wood, but seemed to be cast from glass.

"Nearly there," Cookie said as she wheeled past him to catch up with François.

"Nearly where?" Paul shouted back. He was amazed that he could speak at all. In life he would have been a panting, side-aching mess by now. Yet in death, it seemed his endless summer holidays of running or cycling for miles had returned.

She did not answer, but skated on faster around the next bend and out of sight. He heard François shout an expletive in French. Paul peeked behind him, but could see nothing following him. He felt alone on the stretch of strange road, so he picked up his sprinting pace.

He rounded the corner to find François and Cookie standing dead still in the centre of the perfect road. The surface was not asphalt or concrete. It was some dense, slicker-looking material, he had never encountered before. Yet all thoughts of roads went out of his mind when he looked past his two companions.

There seemed to be a tear in the air in front of them all. Starting at a point eight feet above the road surface and coming down like the pages of a book that had been torn apart. The edges of the tear were deep scarlet and the insides of the rough triangular opening were pulsing red and pink. The heat coming from it was humid and made the air around them feel damp.

"Do I dare ask what it is?" Paul moved forwards to stand beside François and Cookie. The humid air came from the gash in waves.

"It looks like a big moule to me," François commented.

"What it is, boys, is our ticket out of here." Cookie crossed her arms and leant on her left side.

"We have to go through there?" Paul asked as he wiped the sweat from the bridge of his nose.

"What is it doing here?" François flicked his damp hair off his face.

"Who knows who made it or how long ago. The point is it takes us to our next plane and closer to where we want to go."

"You've been this way many times before then?" Paul pulled at his damp shirt that was sticking to his chest.

"A couple of times," she nodded. "Look, it ain't the nicest thing in the world to pass through, but there is no turning back."

Just then there came a roar from behind them, followed by half a tree stump thrown at high speed into the fence at the side of the sloping road. The fence splintered into a million dark, shiny pieces and the road beneath them shuddered.

"Come on," Cookie urged, grabbing their hands and pulling both men with her into the humid, pulsing, damp redness and whatever lay beyond.

CHAPTER NINETEEN

Sam sat on the hard ground with his back to the wall. He wanted to scream with frustration. He looked down at his hands; the skin was ripped to shreds. Two of his fingernails were lost to the stones. There were more scratches than he could count, and he had lost much of the feeling in his left hand. I ain't gonna cry, he thought to himself, I ain't no pussy.

He looked down over the spread of the cemetery that stretched out beneath him. Is this it? Is this hell? An eternity spent trying to achieve the impossible, tortured by the mundane.

A handful of figures picked their way between the graves. Mostly in small groups of two or three or four. It occurred to Sam that for an eternal afterlife the population was sparse, even allowing for the mass of bodies that clumped together as the mob. Okay, so this was only one existence, and on the other side of the wall there was a whole load of other people all having fun in their personal heavens. But still, even if this cemetery was only for those who had killed themselves, there ought to be more bodies.

He thought about asking the kid, and changed his mind. Something about the kid ... it wasn't just the disconcerting effect of speaking to an eight-year-old who had the voice and mind of an old man. The child retained some of the sneaky deceit of a boy. It made him unreliable.

A bell rang, loud and clear across the graveyard. Sam turned and tried to decide where the sound came from, but it seemed to originate from everywhere.

The old woman stood up. "We got a fresh one."

Down on the plain a few of the figures picking their way

between the graves stopped. It was impossible that they could hear the bell all the way down there, and yet Sam had to accept that they had also reacted to the sound.

"Where?" the boy asked.

The old woman closed her eyes and started to turn her body from side to side, like a leaf caught in the wind. Beside her, the old man peered down to the flat pan of the cemetery floor and Sam imagined that this was what they must have been like when they arrived to dig him out of his grave.

The child licked his lips. "A fresh one." He looked down at Sam, seemed to dismiss him, and returned his attention to the old woman. "Where? Where is it?"

She held up a hand. "Hush now. Don't rush me. I got it. I got it."

On the desert floor a lone figure started to run. They were too far away for Sam to make out any details. All he could see was the small dot scampering between the headstones.

A group over to the left shifted direction.

"There," the woman said. She pointed to a spot in the middle of the cemetery. It was partway between the single running figure and the group.

"We could still make it," the old man said.

The child shook his head. "From up here?" He cast a glance at Sam, as if he was to blame for the fact that they were so far from the action.

Sam counted four different groups now, all moving toward the same point. At the edge of the graveyard, the mob turned like a slow wheel, a clump of bodies thousands strong. It started to move in the direction of the new arrival. Achingly slow. It was the furthest away and it crawled toward the spot where everyone else was headed.

"You're going to let them have it?" the old woman asked.

The boy shrugged. "We can't get into a fight now." He turned and addressed Sam directly. "You were lucky we got to you first."

"Sure."

The boy raised an eyebrow. "You don't think so? You'd have preferred to take your chance with that lot?"

The lone figure arrived at the grave just a moment before the first group. Voices drifted back up the hill. Not strong enough to make out what they were saying, but the tone was unmistakable, claiming dibs. Sam smiled, feeling like the afterlife wasn't that different from the beforelife as far as he could make out. People always needed something to own, something to fight over, and it was usually other people. Whether it was Paul and some guy at the pub fighting over a hot woman, or two gangs of the dead clashing over a suicide, put two people in a room and sooner or later there was going to be a fight.

"I think I could have held my own," Sam said. He looked down at his hands. The skin was ripped to shit. He wondered how long it would take to heal in this place. Faster or slower than normal life?

Another gang arrived at the graveside. It was impossible to make out who was fighting who, and equally impossible to determine who, if anyone, was winning. Sam looked away from the fight for a moment. The mob was still way, way over at the far side of the cemetery. They drifted across the graves.

"Why fight?" Sam asked.

No one answered. They were all enrapt by the action playing out down below. There must have been ten figures involved in the scuffle now, and from the corner of his eye Sam noticed the old man's hands twitch, as if he was desperate to get down there and kick some suicide-ass himself.

"What's so important about a new arrival?" Sam tried again. Still, he got nothing from them.

He stood up. Most of his muscles ached from his failed attempts to climb the wall. For a second, the world tilted on its axis and threatened to dump him back down on the ground again. He was shaky as hell. He had been more sure-footed the time he had walked out of the smoking wreckage of the car, but he was upright, and for now that was all that mattered.

The boy turned his head. "What are you doing?"

"Going down. Getting a better look."

"Are you fucking stupid?" the boy shouted. "Do you not see what they're doing to each other down there?"

Sam's initial intention was to gather his hand into a fist and knock the little bastard's head clean off his shoulders, but he was still just a kid. Or at least he looked like a kid, and that was enough to hold Sam for the few seconds it took to reconsider his approach.

"You're not going down," the boy said.

"Says who?"

"You're ours now," the old man said. "You do what we tell you."

"Yours?" Sam said. "You don't own me."

"You think?" the boy asked. His voice carried a quiet tone of menace. The child couldn't hurt him. Could he? Sam tried to laugh it off, the kid only came up to his waist. If he tried to throw a punch, he could hold him out of arm's reach and those pudgy little fists would not even get close to landing a blow. And yet… The way he'd spoken: absolute certainty.

There was a glint in the child's eye. A look that suggested he had been through this before many times and it was Sam who was the younger one now.

"If you go down there you leave my protection," the child said. He sounded like some 1950s East End gangster.

"And?" Sam asked.

"And they'll rip you apart."

CHAPTER TWENTY

Paul stared up at the thin wispy clouds in the pale-blue sky wondering where he was and how he got there. He was lying on the top of a hill, embedded in its knee-length soft green grass. He didn't want to move, only to breathe in the scent of apple and roses that wafted in on the slight, warm breeze.

The clouds were frail and drawn out, making them easy targets for his imagination to turn them into recognisable shapes. A dog's head, followed by a single-winged dragon, mutated into a woman's body. Paul smiled, a look of contentment on his face. His eyelids were leaden and half-closed. The cloud that looked like a woman itched a memory at the back of his mind, but nothing was forthcoming.

The grass was the brightest green he'd ever seen. Its stems were over a foot long, ending in the softest willowy feathers. The acres of them on the hill where he lay cried out perfection to his dulled mind. The warm wind on his face and the aroma of flowers and fruit made him close his eyes for a few seconds. Paul suddenly squinted and wrinkled up his nose and forehead as an image flashed across his mind's eye like a comet. It was an image of a woman with very large hair.

Paul's eyes flicked all the way open again. He squinted against the warm glare of the sun. Something had forced his eyes open, but he could not recall what it was. He raised his head only to find it was far more of an effort than it should have been. He pulled back his arms to use his elbows as leverage. His hands gripped the trampled grass near his body to help pull himself up into a sitting position. He got halfway when his head swam and black dots like a hundred flies appeared before his eyes.

His eyes closed again to shut out the spinning world of exploding miniature black supernovas. Again, the images flashed behind his eyes like film negatives. Firstly of trees flying through the air in a snow-covered world and then the image of him and two others running for their lives.

Paul's eyes snapped wide open again as he sat up in the long, soft grass. The warm breeze across the top of the hill tried to coax him to lie back down again. For some reason he thought of snow, but there was no snow anywhere in the countryside where he lay. He was glad he had sat up though: the view down the sloping hillside was breathtaking. There were swathes of blue, red, and white flowers, that merged together to make a colour palette any artist would be proud of. He thought about lying down again, but his interest was piqued by the colourful blooms.

He stood up before his mind and body had time to reject the idea. He swayed on his ankles for a bit, but stayed on his feet. A sound drifted in the breeze. It sounded to Paul like an infant or child crying. He trudged down the hill, his head heavy as a bowling ball. His footsteps seemed too light, like his legs might crumble under his weight at any second. Yet the momentum of the walk down the hill pushed him forwards. His movements were languid and his arms hung limply at his sides.

He reached the lower part of the hill, where grass met the blue, red, and white flowers. Paul looked along the wild fields of flowers, which seemed at odds with his mind. Surely someone would have to have planted them to get three sets of coloured flowers in their correct bunched positions.

He stopped. Now all he wanted to do was lie down again among the blue flowers. The energy, like a dynamo built up on his trudge down the hill, was now seeping out the soles of his shoes. He was about to give in to those warm fuzzy urges and sleep when he heard a grunt and then a female cry somewhere past the blue flowers. He turned right and walked onwards, skirting the edge of the large field. A girly giggle directed his inner navigation towards the field of white flowers. A perfume, like aloe vera, rose from the white flowers as he brushed past them. Deeper and deeper he went, cutting a swathe through the white flowers.

As he neared the centre, the scent cleared his mind, but also made him smile from one ear to the next. Then, no more than ten feet ahead, a pair of legs stuck up in the air. Each one had a roller skate on it. Paul heard a sudden female inrush of air and a grunt like someone in pain.

Cookie! Paul's mind cleared. He shouted and rushed forwards to help her. He ran on into a small, flattened clearing of trampled flowers and stems to see a small white bum going up and down between Cookie's smooth, dark thighs.

"Do me, Frenchie!" greeted him as he came to a full stop in the clearing. The sight he saw there was more terrifying than anything he'd ever seen in his journey through the afterlife.

CHAPTER TWENTY-ONE

The mob was still a good distance away from the action, Sam noticed. It moved so slowly that by the time it arrived, everything would be over. ZombieGhosts, Sam named it in his head. Because they were all ghosts, right? They were all dead and shuffling around on this B-movie backlot for a 1950s Western, so that made them ghosts. But the horde was something different. The horde was a mindless blob wandering across the ground and presumably sucking up anyone who was too stupid to stay out of the way.

He wondered if there was something inside the middle shouting orders, or whether the delay was the time it took for everyone to agree what they were going to do. Whatever the reason, they were going to be late to the party. Even while he watched, two more groups drifted into the fight.

He looked back at the kid. It was getting easier to hate him. To hate his arrogant way of throwing out orders and expecting them to be followed. Maybe he had been around this place longer and had picked up a few things. Sam thought of a phrase his dad used to say: Who died and left you in charge? And then he started laughing.

"What is it?" the boy asked. His face turned into a snarl. "What's so funny?"

"I get it now," Sam said.

"Sure you do. You get it," the boy snarled his words in a poor imitation of Sam's accent. "You're Mr Knowitall, who only has to hang around trying to climb a wall for ten minutes and then suddenly he gets it."

"You don't want me to go down there because you don't

want me to talk to anyone else."

"You're ours," the old man said. "We found you. We dug you out of the ground. You're ours."

The boy held up his hand and the old man fell silent. When he spoke, his voice was low, and Sam wondered if he was deliberately trying to sound more menacing. "Go down if you want. No one is stopping you. I couldn't hold you back if I wanted, and these two…" he shrugged. "They couldn't stop a charging rabbit. I don't want you to go down there because I've seen what happens to people who get involved. I wanted to save you from that. We pulled you from the ground so that you might stand a chance in this place, but if you want to throw that away, then go for it."

Sam stared at the boy, trying to measure the sincerity of his words.

"Go on," the boy urged. "If you hurry, you can probably get down in time for the finale." His lips curled into a grin, one Sam recognised from before.

"Yeah," the old man muttered. "The finale."

Sam wanted to ask what he meant but decided against it. "I'll go then," he told them. He noticed the stubborn tone creeping into his voice, the one that he had used to tell Paul that he was going to drive because it was his car and he was the better driver anyway. If he thought about it for a minute, he was able to connect that tone with any number of stupid things he'd done during the course of his life. Flipping that car, that was the big one, but it was far from the only one. Walking out of Mr Johnson's maths class because he refused to hand over a note from Trish. Walking out of his job because the foreman turned down his request for a day's holiday. Just one fucking day but it had been too much. That stubborn tone that took over his voice and pushed him where he shouldn't go.

If he took a minute, he would have recognised it, so Sam didn't give himself the chance and instead walked away from the trio who had pulled him from the ground. He didn't look back. He closed his ears to whatever the boy was calling after him. Words of advice, he thought, rather than curses. But he didn't want to hear because he had made up his mind.

He looked down at the mass of bodies roiling at the bottom of the hill. What exactly were they doing down there? What was all the fuss about? A voice in his head suggested that he would find out soon enough.

He had reached the halfway point of the hill before he dared to pause and turn around. The three of them still stood under the shadow of the wall. From this distance Sam could see what an idiot he'd been to try and climb it. Maybe there was a top. There had to be a top, but he would never have reached it, not if he'd kept on climbing all year.

The three of them were watching him, he was sure of that. They were too far away for him to see their faces, but he knew they were standing there and passing judgement on his rash decision to head down to the fracas.

He wanted to return to them, but to do that would be to admit that he had been wrong. He gritted his teeth against the idea. They would make his life hell if he went back. They would remind him every time he tried to offer a suggestion.

Who was it that had told him: A changed mind is a weak mind. His dad? Paul?

Sam shook his head. No, not Paul. Paul had been too bright to fall for something as dumb as that.

And while he argued with himself, he kept on walking. As he got closer to the floor of the cemetery, he heard voices rising up from the huddle. Shouts and cries.

Can I really get hurt? he wondered. He looked down at his hands. The scratches from his attempt to climb the wall were still clear on his skin. *Can I stay hurt?*

Words battered the air, shouted in different languages. Some he understood, spoken in a range of accents from English to American to Indian. Others he recognised by their lilt, and even if he didn't know what was being said he had enough information from the way it was being shouted to make a good guess.

Getting closer to the mob was like leaning into a spinning blade. He knew it was dangerous; he felt the rush of wind against his face. His stomach cramped with nerves and he imagined all the hairs on his arms and neck standing upright. He wasn't afraid, he told himself he wasn't afraid, but only an idiot would ignore the danger of getting close to the pack.

Somewhere in the middle of all those bodies was a new victim. Someone just like he had been a few hours earlier. The latest arrival in the cemetery.

The pack of bodies was too dense to see through to the centre of the mob where the action was happening; all he could make out was the people fighting against each other at the edge.

He wondered why his arrival had not been met by a similar frenzy. Had he not been worth the effort? Had the kid and his sidekicks managed to get him out before anyone else knew he had arrived? It was possible he would never know the answer.

Somewhere in the heart of the mob a scream erupted. People scattered, as if someone had dropped a bomb in the dead centre of the ruckus. He was still a good distance from the action, far enough away that even when the pack disbanded, they came to a halt some distance short of the spot where Sam had paused.

In the middle of the graveyard was an open burial plot. Mounds of brown grave dirt rose up from the edges. There was a small contingent left crowded around the headstone: three women and one man. Sam assumed they had come to the fight together and now emerged as the victors. Members of other groups milled at an invisible boundary as if testing for a way to get back to the graveside.

The three women started a chant. It reminded Sam of a hymn from a church service he had attended. Something about the way the words lifted and fell. He could imagine a pack of monks sitting in their stone cells in an abbey somewhere chanting the same hymn.

A hand rose from the pit. It scratched at the graveside, clawing grooves into the mounds of loose dirt.

The three women dropped to their knees. They reached down into the grave and pulled the body free. It was a young man, not much older than Sam himself. For some reason he expected to recognise the arrival, but the face was that of a stranger.

The young man pulled himself up onto his knees and looked around at the group that had rescued him. He screamed as the first woman scratched her nails across his face, then grabbed him by his hair and began to bash his skull against his headstone.

Sam felt a hand fall on his shoulder.

CHAPTER TWENTY-TWO

"Really?" Paul sat on the grass, with his arms crossed, a bemused look of shock and anger on his eternally young face. "That's what you're sticking to?"

"Well, it is zee truth," François hissed as he bent down into Paul's face and clicked his fingers within an inch of his nose. "Whether you believe it or not."

"The flowers…" Paul began and then cleared his throat loudly in an obtuse manner. "The flowers told you to fuck?"

"It's the way of the world here, sugar," Cookie said to him. She was standing to his left, her hands on her hips in a pose that Paul had become accustomed to seeing. What he hadn't got his head around was her and François writhing around in the dirt, joined at the genitals.

"And what world may that be?" Paul threw his hands up in the air in a confused state. One moment they had been running from some lumbering hulk of a snow-capped monster like something out of one of Lovecraft's most lurid nightmares. The next, they had run through some vaginal-shaped opening into a world of rolling green hills dotted with patches of vibrantly coloured flowers.

"This is the afterlife of flowers and grass, hun."

Paul looked at her and laughed sarcastically. Then he saw the frowns on François's and Cookie's faces and his jubilant mockery ebbed into whispers. "You're being deadly serious, aren't you?"

"For everything there is a season, a time for every activity under heaven." Cookie and Paul turned to François, who had his hand on his heart as he quoted from the Bible.

Paul groaned, put his hands over his eyes, and lay back in the soft fragrant grass. He was not sure he knew what was going on anymore. This trip to save his brother's lost soul was now descending into farcical madness. Was he jealous of François's lucky moment of lust? They had been friends since he'd died, and no one had come between them before. Or was it the lack of movement towards the ultimate goal of finding Sam? They seemed to be *getting nowhere fast,* as his mother used to quote like it was scripture. He certainly had no obvious sexual feeling towards Cookie, even though he'd stared at her chest a few sneaky times. He just felt frustrated about everything. He was doubting the wisdom of going after Sam at all.

"Are you sad because you missed out on the fucking?" François said, falling to a heaped sitting position next to his friend.

"Always room for one more, kitten," Cookie purred as she jiggled her ample chest at him.

Paul saw her wiggle through the fingers he had over his eyes. The thought of a ménage à trois with his companions wasn't helping his confused mood.

"Nooo," he replied, sitting up and hugging his knees. "It's … it's just we don't seem to be getting anywhere."

"Sorry, sugar, this place kinda sends you mad, you know what I mean. I was alone here last time, so this lady didn't get no down-below urges. Then the flowers sorta whispered to me about opening petals and pollination and one thing led to another. Sorry we left you on a hill though." Cookie moved closer and somehow made sitting down wearing roller skates graceful.

"So how do we get to Sam?" Paul knew he had to move the subject on now and try and get the quest going again.

"The red flowers whispered we must head through the Woods of Hell," she replied, giving his hand a squeeze. "I'm hoping that's lost in translation."

"I hope so," François said, scratching at his groin absently. "It does not sound very encouraging."

"So where are these Woods of so-called Hell then?" Paul exhaled, wondering if any woods in the realms of the post-death were nice, happy places full of cuddly bears and picnic baskets.

"Two hills over." Cookie pointed behind Paul's head. He turned his neck as much as he could but saw nothing except the rise of the green slope behind them. "The blue flowers went there once, many did not return."

"Now hold on a fucking minute," Paul shouted. "The *flowers* can *walk*?"

"Yes, but only at night."

"What was I thinking?" Paul said standing up. "Of course, nocturnal migrating blue flowers. Let's go then, before I lose what's left of my mind." He began to climb the green hill as his friends helped each other up.

They followed him. Up the hill and down the next into a valley of yellow, orange, and green daisies. There was a scent of pineapples and cinnamon as they walked through the flowers and up the other bank. His friends managed to catch up and they crested the next hill together and stopped dead at once.

The hill sloped down to a small dell, where the grass waned and only black pulverulent dirt was visible. A V-shaped opening was cut into the bank of the far side of the dell. The blackened earth spread out from the ground up the sides of the banks like a disease. It wasn't this that stopped them in their tracks though, but the sight of the two trees with blackened bark that guarded either side of the entrance. The trees were upside down. Their black leaves and branches half stuck in the dark earth. The roots, bleak and caked in dirt, pointed up to the sky, red dancing flames crackling and burning from them.

"So the Wood of Hell then." François whistled.

"Holy crap," Paul stated.

"Are you sure you want to go on, Paul?"

"Not really Cookie, but I have no choice."

Slowly the three companions trudged down the grassy slope and into hell.

CHAPTER TWENTY-THREE

"Stay," a voice whispered into Sam's ear. "Watch."

Sam turned. The boy only came up to his ribs and yet somehow he exuded authority. His fingers clamped tight on Sam's forearm. Sam thought he could probably take the child in a fair fight, but with the old woman and the man standing nearby, he got the sense that a fair fight was not going to be an option.

"You wanted this, so stay and watch," the boy said.

"No," Sam said. He pulled away from the child, but the fingers remained latched to his arm.

"Don't make me hurt you," the child whispered. To Sam it didn't feel like an idle threat, even though the idea of this small thing causing him any damage should have been a joke. And anyway, he was already dead, what more could the boy do to him?

A sound from the grave seized his attention. Sam whipped his head around. He was in the middle of the group that had claimed him. Claimed—that felt right. They had managed to beat off all the others to stake their claim on this latest arrival and now they were busy ripping him apart.

Is that what they would have done to me? Sam wondered. He stole a glance, but when he turned, he discovered the child was not looking at the scene but rather at him. His grey eyes shone.

What? Sam wanted to ask him. *What do you want from me?* But he kept silent, and when the boy nodded his head, he returned his attention to the open grave.

Two of the women were holding the young man's legs while the third woman and the man held him by the wrists. They stretched him over the grave, pulling him into an X shape. The man had stopped screaming and Sam assumed the blood rushing from the cracked side of his head probably had something to do with his silence. Head wounds bled a lot. He knew that from too many cop shows watched late at night, but the amount of blood dripping onto the ground and staining the soil suggested that the man had more than a scratch.

"Is he dead?" Sam asked.

"Watch."

Sam wanted to turn away. There was something about the way they pulled at the body that was unsettling. It was torture, plain and simple. The man was silent, his head dropped backwards, and Sam wondered if he was already dead. He laughed at himself—of course he was dead, that was why he had been in the grave, that was why they were all there—and then stifled the sound as it came out close to hysteria.

He tried to console himself with the thought that whatever the three women and the man did to him, it was just a hunk of meat, a lifeless body. It didn't mean anything if he couldn't feel it.

And then the young man lifted his head and screamed. He opened his mouth to let out the sound and Sam was sure he heard the tendons in the man's jaw crack. The sound wasn't human, wasn't even vaguely human. It travelled through the air and passed through him, and Sam felt like he had been violated, that the sound had been able to touch something within him that had previously been dormant.

He licked his lips and took a step closer to the grave. The fingers on his arm tightened and sent a flash of pain through his muscles. He didn't need the boy to tell him what was bloody obvious: don't get any closer, don't get involved. He'd seen it often enough when he had been alive—an argument outside a pub on a Friday night. If you tried to step in and intervene, you'd get a jagged bottle in your face before you could say A&E.

The young man's head dropped again and still the four of them kept pulling at his body. Blood gushed from his scalp and into the grave. Sam wondered if there was much fluid left in his body, it seemed like he had already leaked everything onto the ground around him.

He lifted his head again, but there was no energy in him this second time, no passion. He opened his mouth to scream but the only sound that emerged was a high whine like a boiling kettle.

There was a click, like a switch being thrown. When he heard it, Sam had just enough time to think that it was strange, before a red light flashed from the young man's body. A column of light spread out from his chest and enveloped the grave and the four people surrounding him. They dropped his body and Sam thought he heard the thud as the man fell to the ground, landing back in the grave from which he had been rescued.

Sam looked away but it didn't make any difference. He could feel the light burning his skin. It was like standing in the direct fire of a sunlamp turned up to maximum. Even when he clamped his eyes closed against the light he could still see through his eyelids, and he was sure he saw four specks of darkness representing the four people in the heart of the beam.

Someone was chanting. Their voice rose up through the silence. First just one voice and then many. The boy standing beside Sam picked up the words and began to murmur them under his breath, and then the old woman and the man were calling out, too.

"He is Coming. He is Coming. He is Coming. He is Coming."

Who? Sam wanted to ask, but he was too afraid to say anything. It was like he had somehow tripped into an old-style revivalist meeting, and any second now he was going to be pulled on stage by the preacher and told that he must repent his sins or face the wrath of The Lord. Who was Coming. Who was Coming.

"Who is Coming?" Sam whispered. He had to raise his voice to make himself heard, even though the words were directed at the child standing beside him. "Who is Coming? Who is Coming?"

"He is Coming. He is Coming!" the child shouted, and Sam joined in.

"He is Coming! He is Coming!"

The world trembled and Sam did not need to have this explained to him. He was here.

CHAPTER TWENTY-FOUR

He is coming!

Paul was lying on the cold ground. He opened his eyes, or thought he had. He could see nothing but blackness. He blinked hard several times, but it did not help rectify his loss of sight. He closed his eyes and held them shut and counted in his head to ten. The words that had split his skull like a lightning bolt and felled him still echoed around his mind.

He is coming!

He had to force himself not to open his eyes before the count was complete. He opened his eyelids once more, only to discover pressing darkness surrounded him. He pushed himself up, fully expecting to hit the inside lid of a coffin, but the thud of wood on the back of his head never came. He waved his arms around in front of him and he felt the slight noise of their cutting through the chill air, but could see nothing of their passing.

"Paul… Paul, where are you?" François's voice called from somewhere ahead and to the left in the umbra darkness.

"Paulie the Passenger, holler out, darling, so we can find you honey-child." Cookie's voice sounded remarkably close by. Just to his right.

He went to call to her, but cried out in pain instead as one of her roller skates ran over the two smallest fingers of his right hand. He snatched it back and wafted it in the darkness. He was hit by Cookie's Chanel No. 5 perfume, then her hands as she knelt down and pulled him into her heaving bosom.

"I found him, I found him," she cried to François. "You okay, m'man? You gave us quite the fright."

"Curse this impenetrable darkness," François called. "Where are you both?"

"I'm okay," Paul whispered into Cookie's bushy mass of hair. "What happened to me and where are we?"

"Where the bloody-fucks are you twoooooo?" Just then François walked into the embracing Cookie and Paul. He fell over, twisting and landing in a tangle of arms. "Merde."

"Right here, bozo," Cookie hissed as the tumbling Frenchman bashed her right ear as he fell.

"Sorry," he apologised as they all struggled to extricate each other and sit up in a small, close triangle shape.

"Hold hands so we don't lose each other again, okay," Cookie said, reaching out and managing to grab both the men's hands as they sat in the complete darkness.

"Are you okay, mon ami?" François gave his friend's hand a quick double squeeze.

"Yes, I think so, but what happened to me?" A recent memory came to him. "Are we still in that dark, upside-down forest?"

"I'm not sure, sugar. We were all holding hands walking through the woods, when the path suddenly turned totally black. I'm talking beyond brother and sister black. I'm talking total utter night. Then you fell suddenly and started saying, *he is coming*, over and over again."

"Oh god, yes, the dark path. I remember now. I'm not sure who *he* is, but my brother is in deep trouble. We have to leave now." Paul stood up, making his friends scramble to their feet smartly.

"Easier said than done," François said.

Paul turned his head this way and that, knowing that his friend's faces were somewhere to his left and right, yet he could see nothing of them or of his own body. The blackness around him was total.

"Any clues, Cookie?" Paul asked in the direction her gentle breath blew on his right cheek.

"Nope, but I now know how Stevie Wonder feels," she said, her voice lowering with each word she spoke. "I told you boys, I've never been this way before. The green flowers took me a completely different way last time."

"Oh great, we are *done in* by lying flowers," François mocked.

"Well, we can either stay here a while and see if it gets lighter..." Cookie suggested.

"Hate that plan!" Paul interjected.

"Or hold hands and pick a goddam direction and just walk."

"Looks like walking into the night it is," François said, and sighed loudly through his nose.

They lined themselves up as best they could and set off into the darkness, arm in arm. The ground underneath was level and had no grass or debris underfoot. They could not hear, see, or feel anything. They took every step with a nervous trepidation, wondering if the ground would still be there, or if a black abyss would send them tumbling into the darkness.

Paul tried to think of his brother and the near-telepathic thoughts they shared when they were both alive. Maybe in death that would return. Paul wished it so, like a prayer. He thought of his twin brother, conjuring his face in his mind's eye. It was difficult to pull his image from his mind. The surrounding darkness did not help. It conjured up primal fears of what monsters the world may hold.

Paul blinked five times in a row, just to make sure his eyes were open. A long distance ahead there was a smudge of light in the darkness. Paul blinked five times again, wondering if it might be some neural flash on the back of his retina.

"I see something," François whispered. He sounded scared.

Paul felt the hairs on his neck and arms go rigid, like a cold breeze had blown over them.

To his right, Cookie hissed. "I see it, too. It's coming closer, and fast." Her grip on Paul's right hand tightened until it began to hurt.

The football-sized object raced towards them at breakneck speed.

The pale thing came closer, until they could make out the glow of a small face.

No, not a face, but a white, eyeless skull.

CHAPTER TWENTY-FIVE

"Kneel," a voice demanded. It took Sam a moment to recognise that it came from inside him and not from anyone standing nearby. "Kneel in the face of *He who is Coming*."

The light burnt. Even when he clapped his palms over his eyes the red light burnt through him and scratched at his eyes. The world was a confusion of dark shapes. A high-pitched whine, like a fan belt slipping on an old truck, pierced the air.

Sam dared to take his hands away from his eyes. It was impossible to see anything. White light blanketed the world. A white light that burnt and cleansed, bleaching everything it touched. Beneath it he could feel the small boy's fingers still digging into his arm and if he looked hard, he could make out shapes amongst the brightness. He thought he could see the four people standing over the grave holding the body of the dead man between them.

They killed him, Sam thought. For some reason the realisation terrified him—the idea that in this place it was possible to die. Really die. He knew it shouldn't make any difference, because when he'd stepped off that chair and felt the noose tighten around his neck that was what he had expected—a rush into oblivion. Now he knew that death wasn't the end, and now that he knew that Paul was out there somewhere, the idea of really dying was the most terrible fate possible.

He had a million questions to ask but for now the only thing that mattered was that *He* was here. Sam could feel *His* presence—the weight lay on his chest, making it impossible to breathe.

The light grew brighter and hotter. Sam felt the skin on his face burning and he thought that if he got out of this alive, he was going to end up with the worst sunburn in history.

He bowed his head and sneaked a look around him. The man and the old woman had taken on a similar posture beside him. The boy was out of his view, but Sam was sure he was also on his knees. All around him the people who had just been fighting over the new arrival were kneeling down, heads bowed.

Who is this guy? Sam thought.

The light grew brighter again. It reminded Sam of a lightbulb just before it was going to blow. A pulse of pure white light shot though everything. Someone screamed and their voice was cut silent. There was a low hum that burst into words. "He has come. He has come. He has come." And Sam discovered that he was murmuring along with everyone else, under his breath at first, but then he grew in confidence and he was shouting. Beside him, he heard the boy's shrill pre-pubescent voice screaming out the same message.

Sam's vision was a field of pure white. And still it grew brighter. Stronger. Hotter.

"He has come. He has come."

Sam screamed along with the others, the words ripped from his throat. It hurt to speak and yet he could not stop himself any more than he could stop himself from breathing.

"He has come. He has come."

And then the light stopped.

Sam collapsed into a heap on the ground. He felt a chasm open within him and his first coherent thought was a cry of terrible loss.

In front of him most people were struggling to rise to their feet. A few men and women were openly weeping. There was a hollowness to the world that rang within Sam like a dull bell.

In the centre of the crowd was the grave. Or rather, Sam noticed immediately, was the place where the grave had been. The hole had been filled in with brown soil and the headstone was missing. The group of four who had pulled the young man from his coffin was nowhere to be seen.

The sense of rage that Sam had tasted in the air leading up

to the young man's murder was gone. In its place was a tang of ozone, like the air after a lightning storm.

Groups began to drift away from the spot. They left as they had arrived—in small knots only three or four strong. Their shoulders were rounded and their chins dropped to their chests. A few were still crying, wiping tears from their eyes. They staggered away from the gravesite without any sense of purpose or direction.

The boy took Sam's arm and tugged. Sam shook it off.

"We need to go," the boy said.

"No."

"They'll be here soon." The boy's words held a tremor of fear.

"What just happened here?" Sam asked.

"We were visited," the old woman said.

"And the young man in the grave?"

"He's gone."

"Gone?" Sam asked.

"Gone." The word had a hollow ring to it.

Sam shrugged off the boy's hand and moved closer to the grave. He pushed his way past others who were shuffling across the dry ground. They didn't look at him even though just a few minutes earlier he'd had the sense that they would have been happy to rip off his head and pledge it as an offering.

Sam stood beside the fresh earth of the grave. There was no sign of the teenager or any of the four that had been there. He could feel their absence.

"Where are they?" he asked.

"We have to go," the boy said to Sam. He looked up and Sam followed his gaze to a point just short of the horizon where the mob shuffled their steady way toward them.

"They come to feed on what is left behind," the old woman said. "And if you're still here, then they will feed on you, too." She moved away, up the hill, just a few steps, and then stopped to see if the others followed. The man hurried to catch up with her, but the boy remained hanging steadfast to Sam's arm.

"See?" the boy said.

Sam shook his head. He didn't see anything. He didn't

understand anything and yet the boy acted like everything was now obvious.

"I'm not going anywhere until you explain what happened," Sam said.

The boy's eyes widened. Over his shoulder Sam could see the people moving slowly away from the spot on which he stood. He thought he could feel a tremble in the air like the last vestiges of a storm rumbling away, but maybe that was nothing but his own imagination.

"You really want to do this now?" the boy asked.

Sam nodded. Once. Sharply. He didn't know if he did. He felt the unease and he was aware that the mob was somewhere behind him, out of sight. He was confident he didn't want to be standing there when they arrived to hoover up whatever was left behind.

"Where is the man? What happened to him?"

"He's gone," the boy said. His voice flat and emotionless. He might have been telling Sam they had just missed the bus.

"Where?"

"He's just ... gone. Like he never existed."

"Can that happen?"

"It's what we saved you from."

Sam noticed the anger in the boy's voice but chose to ignore it. "And the others ... the ones who killed him. Where are they?"

"Gone," the boy said. But there was something about the way he said the word, as if it had a different meaning. As if their gone was different to what had happened to the poor soul they had dragged from the grave. And his voice...

Sam thought about it for a moment and realised he didn't want to alert the boy to the idea that he had noticed anything. "All gone," Sam murmured to himself.

"And we will be, too, if we don't get out of here soon."

Sam looked at the boy. He was getting used to looking beyond the childlike face and reading something of the older expressions written on the plump features. He allowed the boy to drag him away from the graveside. They moved along the terrace rather than heading back up the hill toward the great wall. He wondered where the boy was taking him, because now he was no longer naïve enough to think that the boy was simply dragging him away from the grave. He was taking him somewhere. Because the child had a plan, an agenda. Sam had seen it: the calculating way he had tried to mask how he really felt, a level of deviousness that a true child could never manage.

What do you want from me? Sam wondered. His mind brought forward the face of the teenager as he emerged from the grave.

The boy, who had seemed to be nothing more than a child when Sam had first encountered him, allowed any pretence to fall from him. When Sam paused to look behind, he saw the mob had arrived—a huge mass of people walking in a large circle around the centre point of the grave. He shuddered and allowed the child to drive him onwards.

CHAPTER TWENTY-SIX

They could not see to flee, so they stood and cowered on the chilly ground, staring as the bare white skull approached them.

It stopped five feet before them. The size of three human skulls put together and knitted into one huge bony countenance, malevolence seemed to exude from it in waves, swallowed up by the surrounding impenetrable darkness. Yet for its unnatural size it had no outwardly supernatural menace; there were no glowing eyes, no skeletal body, just a skull and a jaw, floating six feet above ground.

It hovered, like it was appraising them, yet its eye sockets were black pits, which could easily fit a cricket ball. Paul was frozen in a half-standing position. Cookie was to his left, kneeling as she clung to his funeral-suit trousers. François on the other side felt like he was even lower to the unseen ground. Maybe even flat out on the cold floor.

Paul took a deep breath and rose to his full height—level with the empty nose hole of the giant skull. Paul figured it could be part of some elaborate trap to keep away nosey travellers. He surmised that behind the skull would be a pole or ropes holding the inhuman skull aloft. Paul gulped loudly and moved a couple of inches towards the hovering white manifestation. He felt both his companions grab his legs to hold him back.

His slight movement caused a reaction. The lower jaw fell suddenly open, showing only the blackness behind the huge skull. Then it let out a scream, so sudden and so ear-splitting it knocked the startled Paul off his feet in sheer fright. He fell backwards. His two companions cushioned his fall, as they also scrambled backwards from it. The skull had no larynx to tire, nor any burning lungs to fail. It screamed at a constant high-pitched rate. All the three companions could do was writhe in agony on the floor as they clamped their hands over their ears, but the falsetto screeching could not be stopped by hands or fingers in the ears. It vibrated through the very bones of each of them. It reminded Paul of when he stood next to a huge bass-bin speaker at a club in Ibiza, in the summer holiday before he met his end.

He could only just focus on the screaming dead skull as tears of pain clouded his vision. The constant screaming felt like icy bony fingers thrust ever deeper into his skull. Then something hit the skull full on and it shattered into three pieces. The screaming stopped in time for them to hear the heavy object hit the ground. The cleaved skull and the detached lower jaw reformed into three identical smaller skulls. The skulls were now human size and floated two feet apart from each other. Their newly formed jaws dropped and began to scream once again, lower in pitch, but now at three times the intensity.

Paul clamped his hands over his ears once more and fell to his right, on top of François, who looked like he was trying to dig a hole in the cold earth beneath them. Paul realised he could see his male friend in the dim glow of the three skulls. He winced as the screams tore through his head. Looking around he could see the edge of the wide forest path now, a long branch and the base of a black tree.

From his dimly lit left something flew at the left-hand skull. It was one of Cookie's skates. It hit the skull dead on, breaking it into four pieces. Paul realised that his female guide was now out of ammunition. The four pieces deformed into four bobbing, smaller, and, it seemed, brighter skulls. They were about the size of a small dog's or a cat's skull. Their jaws dropped open and deeper screams emitted from them.

Paul crawled quickly past his French friend as he felt drips of blood on his earlobes. He could see even more of the left-hand side of the forest of the dead. The path they had set out on in the sunshine, and then utter darkness, carried on behind the glowing skulls. The trees were the colour of cold lava. The roots were unseen on high in the uber-darkness around them. Crucified to each tree trunk, with ebony-coloured iron nails, were the burnt, black remains of corpses.

Paul could see bodies nailed to every tree trunk in this damned forest. His scrambling hands found a large, straight branch, and he charged at the nearest skull and smashed it with the branch end.

"Get moving," he shouted over the screaming as he moved over to the next skull. The bits of the first skull were reforming. Yet their smaller state seemed to enhance the illumination coming from them. He went along, smashing skulls into bits as he went, screaming his own head off to keep out the noise of the skulls.

He saw Cookie drag François to his feet. She pulled him along the path, pausing only to collect her skates. She smashed more as she went past up the path. Paul took two more wild swipes, the skulls so small now they were getting impossible to hit. In the ever-increasing light, he followed his two friends away from the now-baritone screams of the many tiny skulls. The screams diminished as they fled, but the light grew brighter, leading them on, deeper into the Wood of Hell.

CHAPTER TWENTY-SEVEN

"We won't have to worry about them for a while," the child said.

Sam watched the writhing mob. Even this far away he felt vulnerable, as if the sprawling mass of bodies could still catch and engulf him. And what then? It was impossible to know what went on within the core of that mob, but he was happy to assume that it was nothing he wanted to be part of. He realised that in his head he heard the smacking sound of jaw bones clattering together as they ate, and even though he didn't know what might be there for them to consume, Sam was confident his instinct was right.

"Where are you taking me?" he asked the boy.

"Away."

"I need to find my brother."

The boy turned around and charged back at Sam until he stood in front of him. "Don't you get it? You're stuck here. We're all stuck here. There is no way out."

Sam stared into the eyes of the boy. He was lying. He didn't know what the truth of the situation was, yet, but Sam knew that the boy was lying. For the first time since he'd been dragged out of his own grave, he felt something close to hope. The boy was lying, which meant there *was* a way out of this hell. It might also mean that the boy knew the way out. He could work with that.

He considered grabbing the boy and bending his arm back until he spilled his secret or the bones in his arm snapped like dry firewood. He could do it. In the right circumstances it could be very effective. The two companions that flanked the boy didn't look strong enough to present a challenge and the boy was just a child, with a child's strength.

The boy stepped back from Sam. His eyes reflected Sam's plan in them. "You need me," he whispered. "If you think you can get out of this place on your own, you'll end up like that kid down there: served up for the Great Creator as an offering."

Sam shrugged. "If that's what it takes."

"I could have done that when I helped you from your grave, if that was what I wanted."

"Don't you want to get out?" Sam asked.

The child's eyes lit up and at first Sam assumed it was anger, but then he understood he was seeing something else in the boy's face: an urge. A passion that ran through him so deeply that when it surfaced, his whole body shivered.

"You can't get out. None of us can," the old woman said.

But the boy's eyes said different. "Do you know how long I've been here?" he asked.

Sam shook his head. The boy frightened him. His eyes shone with anger.

"Five hundred years I've walked this hell hole. I tried climbing the wall. I didn't give up when my fingernails were pulled out and my palms started to bleed. I got high enough that when I fell, it shattered the bones in my right leg and I was left lying on the ground for weeks. I joined the cult and spent a decade hoovering up the dregs from each open grave. I walked to the far ends of the land where there is nothing and no one. I spent a year on my knees staring up at the sky until the sun burnt out my retinas, and still the Great Creator did not take pity on me. And you think I can just click my fingers and whisk us out of here."

"Why didn't you offer me up to the Great Creator in exchange for your release, like those women did just now?"

"Because we don't do that."

Lies. Sam saw it in his eyes, in his whole body. He shifted away from Sam, trying to hide the untruth. The people on either side of him looked equally awkward and Sam realised that this had been their plan. Something had gone wrong, because he was still there. When they had helped him out of his grave, it had only been so he could be sacrificed to the Great Creator as their ticket out of this place.

He tried not to feel angry. He tried to tell himself that after five hundred years he would probably do the same thing. Hell, after five days he would probably offer up anyone he could get his hands on if it meant finding Paul.

"So what do we do?" Sam asked. His voice was calm. There was no hint of the heat he felt. He was proud of his self-restraint and he figured he would need every shred of cunning if he was to survive in this murderous pack long enough to find Paul. When he looked at the three of them now, he no longer saw a child, a man, and an elderly woman. When he looked at them now, he saw three hungry jackals, just waiting for the right time to pounce and rip him to shreds.

Sam nodded his head slowly and wondered whether it was easier to walk beside your nemesis in ignorance or full knowledge. Now he would watch every step he took. He would always sleep with one eye open and be careful never to turn his back on them.

What do we do? he had asked, and he could see the boy considering his response.

"That depends on what you have the stomach for, Samuel Wright."

"Whatever it takes," Sam told him. He shivered; a flash of cold air found him in this hot, dry place. He stared at the boy. Just a boy, he reminded himself. Five hundred years old but just a boy. And he felt like he'd just sold his soul to the devil.

CHAPTER TWENTY-EIGHT

The path through the decayed wood seemed to go on forever. The dull path twisted this way and that through the upside-down trees. The screaming had died away now, far into the distance. They tried to concentrate on the path itself. Eyes cast ahead to see which way it would turn next.

What they didn't do was stare at the trees themselves. Not at the dead burnt bark, bare roots and trunks, or the flames that flickered blood red. They definitely didn't stare at the corpses—burnt flash-fast at some terrifying heat—nailed to each tree in the dead forest. The charred remains of men, women, children, and infants. They must have passed hundreds, if not thousands of them. They were used to them, as far as they could be by now, but the endless rows of burnt bodies had a cumulative effect on the three travellers. Paul wished for the time when it had been so dark he could not see anything. Yet the darkness after the screaming skull attack had lessened. It was like night, but with some ambient light showing them the path.

The tension of keeping his vision fixed on the path, and path alone, was starting to build within him. The burnt corpses nailed to the trees were caught in peripheral vision now and again, making them seem more grotesque. Rows and rows of bent, twisted thin arms and legs. Mouths, wide open in screaming, agonising death throes. The air was heavy with the funk of overcooked flesh.

The trio walked on in total silence, keeping as close together as they dared in the centre of the wide path. When it forked into three separate routes, Paul just pointed with his finger without uttering a word. They walked up the forks and took it in turns to stare down each path. Each different way twisted and turned, lost from sight after thirty feet or so.

"Which shall we choose?" François asked, shrinking into himself a little at the loudness of his own voice in the near silence.

"Haven't a clue," Paul said ducking left and right to see if any of the paths gave any guide. "What do you think, Cookie?"

"They are testing our resolve, boys. Trying harder than ever to freak our shit out."

"I don't think I could get any more jumpy than I am now," Paul stated to no one in particular.

"They are putting doubt before us. We have a hard decision to make. Do we pick one way and all mosey along down it, or each take a path of our own and scout out the best way?" Cookie said, pointing from the left path to the right.

"Stick together," François blurted out quickly.

"Yep, but that's what they are expecting us to do. They think we are three scared babes-in-the-woods. If we are brave, we can each go fifty feet down a separate path, or count to a hundred. When we reach a hundred, turn the fuck around and come back to this point. Always do what your enemy least expects." Cookie's voice was resolute and strong in the dark, silent wood.

"I dunno," Paul said in a dubious tone, looking at the corpse-lined routes ahead of them.

"I do," François nodded feverishly. "We stick together, right?"

"Or we all take each route together for a count of hundred and then return to this point. Then we will know if any of them shows us a route out of this horrible forest," Paul suggested as a safer option to his fellows.

"Or you two pussies could try one way and I'll take one of the others just to save us some time." Cookie was standing with her hands on her hips again. She kicked her right skate against the side of the left one to spin her wheels. The slowing, spinning noise was the only sound in the dark forest. The two men weren't sure what was worse, the burnt corpses impaled on the trees or Cookie's cold, hard stare.

"We could each try a way, I suppose," Paul said, looking down at his shoes.

"Are you two insane?" François bleated. "That sounds like the worst possible thing to do."

"Showing that famous yellow French streak again?" Cookie tutted her erstwhile lover.

"I am as brave as the next person." François pouted and pushed out his chest.

"I am the next person," Cookie said, raising her eyebrows at him. "I'm willing to take a path alone—are you?"

François went to speak, looking up from her chest, to meet her cold, brown eyes. Then he stopped, her withering gaze halting his protests. With a shifty glance at Paul, he nodded twice.

The three of them spread out, each taking the nearest path to them. With a wave, they started off alone down their own paths: Paul the left way, François straight ahead, and Cookie down the right-hand fork. It only took them ten steps before the person to their side was lost from sight. The darkness and the corpse trees soon blocked their view through the dividing paths.

On a tree just to the left of the fork, one of the corpses slowly raised its head from where it was fused to its chest. Black brittle chunks of charred flesh fell from the ripped wound. The corpse's eyes flicked open, revealing white pupils in the centre of two red eyes. She watched the backs of the three companions disappear down each fork. Once they were all out of sight, she began to pull her right hand off the nail with which she was crucified. It came away, leaving chunks of crispy flesh behind.

Then she began to work her left hand free.

Across the path, her opposite counterpart started to do the same.

CHAPTER TWENTY-NINE

"There is a way," the child said. "It is not for the faint-hearted and I only know what I have been told. Obviously, I do not know if anyone has ever been successful, only that the people who have tried it are no longer here."

"Where else would they be?" Sam asked.

"When you killed yourself, where did you think you were going?"

Sam was silent. He didn't like to conjure up the memory of his last few minutes on Earth. It came anyway, as if the boy had found a way to access his thoughts and drag them to the surface. He could feel the scratch of the rough twine around his throat and he clearly remembered worrying that when he stepped out into death, the cord would not hold his weight. He remembered the taste of terror. The way the muscles in his legs melted into string when he tried to take that first step. He could feel it at the back of his throat and taste it in his mouth. For a moment, he was back in the barn praying that no one would find him too soon because he knew he didn't have the courage to make a second attempt.

"Tell me what I have to do."

The child looked around him and then sat down on the spot. For a second, Sam loomed above him and peered down on the top of his head. He was amused to see a small bald ring in the centre of the curly hair, as if this eight-year-old was suffering from male-pattern baldness. The man and the old woman lowered themselves to the ground. Sam was sure he heard the creak of tendons as she settled onto the hard ground.

Finally, Sam sat as well. He looked at his companions: the

child seemed lost in thought; the man and woman peered at him, oblivious to Sam. They looked worried, maybe even afraid. He had an idea that even they did not know what the boy was going to say.

"It has been said that there is no way to leave this world. That this barren landscape is our penance. That may be correct, and it may be our just reward, but that does not stop people striving to escape." The boy spoke in a low, constant voice that was far removed from his normal manner of talking. It made Sam think of a phoney psychic medium at a village fête. He expected the child to ask them to link hands so that they could better communicate with the other side, but at the same time there was a stillness and surety about the boy. His words carried the weight of five hundred years of experience with them.

"I can show you the way," the boy said.

Under the hot sun, Sam felt a chilled wind breathe over him. He looked to his right—the old woman was terrified. *So you feel it too?* he wanted to ask her.

"You have to be ready to sacrifice everything, just as you sacrificed everything to arrive here. For most that is impossible, now that they understand what they have given up."

The boy looked at Sam. "Can you do that?"

Sam nodded. His mouth was too dry to answer.

"Can you do that?" the boy demanded.

"Y-Yes," Sam stammered.

"Can you do that?" the boy shouted.

"Yes!" It was the old man, screaming at the top of his voice. "Yes, I can."

Sam heard the woman beside him whisper, "No," but he didn't think her answer could be heard above the man's shouts.

"Yes," the man called again. "I can do that. I can do anything. I will risk everything to leave this hell."

And still the boy looked at Sam. His eyes seemed to pierce through to Sam's soul and his words spoke directly to his heart.

"Can *you* do that?" he asked quietly.

Sam nodded again, and when he realised that this was not enough, he whispered, "Yes."

The boy smiled.

"Good. I knew I chose well. We will begin."

CHAPTER THIRTY

Even with light coming from somewhere that Paul could not fathom, it was still as dark as a moonless night. He wished he had some flaming brand to hold and scare the frights away and calm his own nerves. Yet he knew from real-life experience that such torches normally screwed up your own night vision and made you a sitting target to every creature under the dark moon. He and Sam used to make them when they were twelve.

Their friend Ali Kabir had found an entrance to some old Second World War bunker on a piece of wasteland owned by his uncle. Ali's uncle had bought it at auction ten years ago, intending to build six houses on it, but there had been some caveat in the deeds forbidding the building of houses on the site for eighty years.

So they had used it as their own private playground. They had found the grate buried under a four-foot sea of grass. Ali had been caught short and popped into the tall grass for a piss. He had stepped on the rusted grate, which broke at one end and had fallen down into the darkness below. Ali had come running back to where they were, pulling up his fly, blood running down from a gash on his right shin. Ali was so excited that he didn't feel the pain and they all rushed over to the now-exposed grate. A corner of the rusty grate was missing, letting the sunlight show a taste of what lay beneath. All they could see as they lay in the tall grass and peered into the depths were rungs of a ladder descending into darkness.

After a quick trip to the twin's garden shed to pick up some sacking and white spirit, they were soon back at the grate. Paul set about making three torches—à la Indiana Jones films—while Ali and Sam used an old washing pole to smash the rest of the cover. The metal rungs headed down into the blackness below. Ali went down first because he had found the grate. He got his head just below ground level when he lost his bottle and hurried back up. Paul, who had no real fear of anything, eagerly scrambled down in his place. Sam, who was the expert with fire and fire-related incidents, lit a torch and handed it down to his twin brother.

Paul dangled off the rung he was on and gripped the torch as low down as he could.

Then he offered it to the darkness.

Instead of revealing where the downward passage went, the flame of the torch flared up at him, so he could see even less than when he hadn't been holding it. He swung it back and forth, but the darkness didn't retreat before the flickering torch. In the end, all he could do was drop it down the man-made hole. The torch only fell another five feet, before landing with a slight splash and a hiss. The light slowly faded to nothing, but not before Paul could see that there was water below.

"What can you see?" Sam called down to him.

"I see that we will have to go home and fetch our wellies," Paul said, climbing back up. They trudged back to their house, fetching a spare pair for Ali who had never possessed a pair of Wellington boots. Using the other two torches for effect and Paul's large silver torch to actually see where they were going, they headed down. The water at the bottom was only two to three inches deep. A long passageway led off in a northerly direction. Its walls were covered with white tiles like a tube station. It ran on for twenty feet or so before coming to a dead end. There were no doors, arches, or side passages and no signs anything had been blocked up. What started as an exciting adventure ended in disappointment. It was dank and cold, and after four more trips over the next fortnight, they got bored and covered up the hole, just in case some small kid or animal fell into it.

Paul realised he had lost count as his mind wandered back to his youth. He reckoned he must have easily counted past two hundred, let alone one, so he turned around and started back down the path. He wondered if the other two had found any better ways out of here. If the other paths were the same, they would have to pick one and hope for the best. He had just rounded a tight corner when he heard a scream. It sounded like François.

He increased his speed into a jog, taking care to stay away

from the edges of the path and the legion of burnt dead hanging from the upside-down trees.

He stopped.

One of the corpses from the trees stepped out of the dark forest ahead and to his left. The sight of the tight muscles in its arms and legs caused a shiver to run through him. Were all the dead in this forest moving? Was this their hell? Paul could not envisage a worse punishment than to be crucified and burnt alive.

As soon as the burnt corpse stepped upon the path, shoots of orange flame spread from its badly melted toes. The fire did not stop the poor unfortunate female; she continued onto the path just ahead of Paul. Flames shot up her other already charred leg, up her torso until she was aflame from head to toe. Reaching out with melted burning fingers, she shuffled towards Paul.

CHAPTER THIRTY-ONE

Sam followed the boy and was in turn followed by the man. The old woman hung at the back, and each time Sam looked in her direction, the distance between her and the rest of them seemed to grow. He wanted to ask her why she was so frightened, but the boy set a fast pace, winding between the headstones with a clear purpose, and each time Sam slowed down to try and let the woman catch up, the boy turned around to castigate him.

"We have to get there soon," the boy called over his shoulder. He increased his pace and Sam matched him. Over his shoulder he heard the laboured breathing of the man struggling behind.

The sun burnt down on them. Sam hadn't noticed at first but now that they were almost running, the air he pulled into his lungs scorched his throat. Quickly his mouth became dry, and though he licked his lips to keep them moist, it made little difference. He felt like all the moisture was being sucked from his body.

The boy started to run. Sam tried to keep up. Sweat lathered his face and arms and fell in coin-sized drops onto the earth. Salted water dripped from his brow and stung his eyes. The distance between him and the boy lengthened.

"Slow down!" he called out. His voice sounded thin and weak in his own head and he wasn't sure if the boy would hear him, but up ahead the figure he was chasing halted.

"No."

Sam felt lightheaded. When he looked out to the horizon, the ground began to shimmer in a heat haze. It looked like the sky and earth were melting.

He tried to slow down but his legs continued the race across the flat land. Fatigue spiked his muscles. Shots of pain lanced into his calves. His heart skipped a beat and then began fluttering as if it was trying to catch up.

Still the boy ran on to the horizon.

When Sam looked behind him now, the man was a speck in the distance, still desperately trying to retain his place in the race. The old woman was nowhere to be seen and Sam wondered whether she had stopped and was now sitting on the edge of a grave somewhere. Part of him envied her decision. He couldn't do that. He couldn't just ignore the boy up ahead and collapse onto the ground. The boy pushed and he followed because he had to, because if he didn't, he would never see Paul again. The thought of that loss, a second and more permanent betrayal, powered the race. His arms pumped by his sides. Running hurt more than he could imagine and yet he could not stop. Would not stop.

He heard the boy's voice in his ear even though it was impossible. The boy was murmuring hushed secrets that explained they were trapped in the land because they chose to be trapped inside the land. The key to their escape was with them all along but people did not have the courage to recognise it.

"Salvation is not found in the agony of others," the boy whispered. "We cannot seek our escape through a cult which scavenges the dregs of other people's pain. We cannot escape through the terror of destruction where we rip the newborns from their graves and offer them up to the Great Creator. I have lived with the cult and found no answer. I have made sacrifices to the Great Creator and received nothing in response except silence.

"This is what we must do," the boy said.

Sam looked behind him. The graveyard was a blurred landscape. The headstones were indistinguishable from the earth. The man was gone. The old woman was gone. The wall was a jagged smear on the horizon, only as tall as a pebble.

"What if you're wrong?" Sam asked.

It was impossible that the boy could hear him. The boy was in the far distance, not even a figure. The boy could not hear him and yet he answered, "If I'm wrong then we …" But before the boy had a chance to finish his sentence, he began to scream.

Ahead of him, Sam saw the sky darken, and although he knew he should be grateful for the relief from the searing heat of the sun, his only thought was terror. Darkness came crashing down upon him as complete as death.

And then in the darkness he saw a flicker of light up ahead, where he thought the boy had been standing. He grew closer, his legs pounding the blackness underfoot and dragging him forward despite his fear. "No," Sam murmured. He tried desperately to halt his progress. It was like running off a cliff into perfect oblivion. With each step he took he expected the ground to fall away beneath him until there would be nothing left.

"No," he shouted, but his muscles pulled and his legs pumped as he covered the distance between him and the flaming boy. The boy screamed.

"Save me, Mother," the boy cried. "Save me, Father. I am sorry. Great Creator, come for me."

As Sam got closer, the stench of burning flesh rose in his consciousness. At first it was a taste at the back of his throat, but as he approached, it became stronger, hotter, until it possessed all his senses. He could see the boy in front of him, consumed by the fire. The boy had stopped running. He was no longer able to move the blazing chunks of meat that had once been his limbs. As Sam approached, the boy turned in his direction.

"Help me," the boy cried.

"How?"

"Kill me."

Sam looked around him. The ground was bare of anything that might be used as a weapon.

He will be dead soon, Sam thought as he stared at the boy. There was nothing left of his body and yet it continued to burn, beyond anything that was physically possible.

"Die," Sam said. "Please die." But the boy lay on the ground and whimpered and cried, and even though there was nothing left of him, he continued to call out to God and his Mother and Sam to help him and deliver him from his agony.

He has to die, Sam thought, and yet he continued to stare and the boy did not die. Could not die. The flames rolled over his body. There were no muscles left on his bones to burn, and so the flames ate away at the calcium and the marrow and burnt with an orange tinge.

After an eternity—hours, weeks, months, years, Sam had no way of measuring the time—he stepped into the flames. He placed his hands around the throat of the boy and he squeezed. Although the flames surrounded him, he did not burn.

He choked the life out of the boy. He stared into his eyes and watched him die. And in the boy's eyes Sam saw not a reflection of himself, but an image of Paul.

CHAPTER THIRTY-TWO

Paul could do nothing but retreat the way he came, away from the rendezvous with his friends. The poor burning creature, enveloped totally in flames, now shuffled in silent agony up the path towards him.

He glanced to the left and right, trying to find any kind of weapon to fend off the burning corpse. To his right he spotted a branch close to the edge of the path. It was about two feet long and charred black, but dead beggars could not be choosers and he reached for it.

He knew something was wrong the instant he picked it up. What he had first thought to be twigs were little fingers that belonged to the severed arm he now held. As Paul brought it across the boundary between the path and forest, it combusted in his hands. He dropped it at once with a shriek. The arm shrivelled and burnt at his feet, yet his hands had felt no heat, nor had the skin of his palms been burnt.

His attention was prised away from the burning arm by the advancing woman, or what was left of her. Her leg had crumpled at the ankle and snapped as she took a step towards him. Her balance went and she fell. As she hit the hard path, her blackened body broke apart. Her left knee shattered, sending ash and charcoal everywhere. Her left arm crumbled beneath her. Her back split open from her buttocks up to her neck.

Paul scrambled back a few more steps and watched in morbid fascination as her neck finally failed and she sank to the ground. It kept going until there was nothing left of her head but a rough circle of black ash.

Paul put his hand to his mouth and gagged. Something

emerged from the deep, long rent in her back. A long, dark shadow of the woman she had formerly been. It seemed to Paul that some invisible hand had grabbed her neck and was pulling her screaming spirit out of her ashen remains. Her body stretched into the darkness above until it became too thin to see.

"Shit," Paul managed to say between hard breaths.

A child's scream pulled him to his senses. He ran, leaping over the woman's crumbling remains, and back down the way he had come. He kept looking at the corpses nailed to the trees, but none of them had moved since he first passed them. He slowed to reach the fork and saw a burning man fall to pieces. Cookie and François were holding each other tight, looking down at the burning man.

François looked up and saw him. Relief flowed over his pale features. He pushed Cookie around the decaying man to where Paul was standing. They all embraced.

"I do not like this place," François said.

"I had one after me, too," Paul said. "She caught on fire as soon as she stepped onto the path."

"Maybe this is how they became all burnt up," François suggested.

"Yeah, but they didn't nail themselves to the trees, did they? Someone or something did that to them," Paul said, looking down at the ash man. Part of his chest fell out and his dark spirit was sucked across the path and into the umbra forest beyond.

"What was that?" François said, holding out both his palms towards Cookie.

She did not answer. She was walking over to the edge of the path, where, earlier, the woman had pulled free her burnt corpse.

"Cookie?" François called to her, but she ignored him. She was leaning towards the upside-down tree. The blackened remains of a child were now nailed to the tree.

"There was a woman here before we went our separate ways," she said over her left shoulder.

"Cookie, my darling, be careful. Yes?" François warned her from where he stood a safe distance away.

Paul walked over to stand next to her. The boy's corpse

looked fresh. Smoke was still drifting up from his burnt clothes, which had fused with his blackened skin.

"You're right, Cookie, he wasn't here before. It was a woman, maybe the same woman who came after me."

"Where did you come from, my poor tortured little man?" Cookie said sadly to the burnt features of the dead boy.

His eyelids flicked open, revealing bloodshot orbs. Paul and Cookie gasped, grabbed each other, and took a step backwards. The boy's eyes fixed on Paul and he could see the pain in the poor young creature's eyes. The boy's lips cracked open. Smoke emanated from his open mouth as he tried to speak. One word croaked from his burnt lips.

"Paul!"

CHAPTER THIRTY-THREE

Sam heard his word echo, as if returned to him. "Paul." In the dying boy's eyes he saw an image of his brother, and his first instinct was to dismiss it as an illusion. He had been through so much over the last twenty-four hours that it was no surprise his mind grabbed at anything and tried to make sense of it.

But it *was* Paul, he was sure of it. His brother was just as he always remembered him: the same untidy black hair, the same flash of anger and intelligence in his eyes. His jaw set hard as if he'd just wandered into an argument.

"Paul. Can you hear me?"

The image in the dying boy's eye was tiny and yet Sam found it easy to see every detail of his brother's face. He'd found him. He'd really found him. He knelt down beside the boy and realised that the child was whispering, his charred lips moving slowly. Sam leaned closer until the boy's lips brushed against his ear, and still his words were so quiet that it was impossible to hear what he was saying.

"What is it?" Sam asked. He wanted to grab the child and shake the words out of him, words that had come from Paul, he was sure of it. But to lay a hand on the smouldering remains of the child would probably cause them to crumble to ash. He held back on the urge to force the words out of the boy and instead listened more intently and tried to pull meaning from the shallow in-out breaths of the child.

He thought he heard his name spoken. Maybe it was just wishful thinking, but it sounded like his name.

"Paul, can you hear me? Are you okay?"

He watched the miniature scene in the child's eye. Paul's

eyes narrowed, as they did when he was concentrating. Sam felt the pull of a smile on his own lips as he recognised the familiar expression of his sibling. He tried not to base too much on that tiny image and yet he could feel his heart swelling with joy. Paul was still alive—he'd been right all along. It was a connection, something that not even death could sever. They were meant to be together and nothing that the boy or the Cult or even the Great Creator himself did would be able to stop that. It was destiny. Fate. Kismet. Call it what you want, Sam knew by looking into the face of his twin that they would be together again.

The boy in front of him whispered and Sam leant closer to listen.

"Sam? Is that you, Sam?"

He nodded. He wondered what was happening on the other side where Paul was. The background seemed dark. Maybe he was trapped in a cellar somewhere, or in a world that was permanently night. The idea of Paul alone in this other dark world, maybe sentenced to remain there from the day they had rolled the car all those years ago, caused Sam's heart to ache. It was all his fault; it was always his fault.

"Don't worry, Paul, I'm coming for you."

Paul blinked.

Sam smiled. He realised he was holding tight to the hands of the dying boy, as if he was holding the hands of his brother. Dry, hot skin under his own. Brittle. Crisp wafers of burnt skin flaked off under his grip.

The boy mewled in pain—his own voice this time, not channelling Paul's flat accent. Sam released his grip on the boy's hand but then noticed that when he did, the image in the centre of his eye faded and so he held tighter. He could hear the boy's pain and was torn between the desire to release him and the need to stay in contact with Paul.

"I'm coming to find you," Sam said.

He thought he saw a smile on Paul's face, an acknowledgement of the promise. He tried not to think of how many promises they had made to each other over the years, and how many of those they had broken as casually and completely as snapping a twig underfoot: I'll look after you; I'll watch your back; I won't sleep with your girlfriend. Sam smiled at the memory because, although it had felt like a betrayal at the time, in hindsight it had been nothing. Hell, he couldn't even remember the girl's name now. It was Paul who was important, Paul who had always been more important than anything else that had happened in his life.

I'll stay with you.

The smile dropped from Sam's lips. Immediately and completely.

"I'm sorry," he said. He watched carefully for the response on Paul's face and wondered if his brother would understand what he was saying.

"I should have stayed. But I was scared."

Just talking about that Friday night caused his body to respond. He knew the heat he could feel was the boy's body burning down, but his mind interpreted it as his memory of waking up after the crash, staring at the stain on the ceiling of the car that always reminded him of a map of Australia. The alcohol washed from his system in a stark moment as he heard his brother's cries. The floor was burning; the rugs set alight by the cigarette Paul had been holding. The fire inside the car burnt with a pale-blue flame and an acrid black smoke.

"I tried," Sam said. In his memory his hands were burnt raw from snatching at the seat belt that trapped his brother in the passenger seat of the car. He was hung sideways and his breath reeked with the tang of beer and cigarettes. Sam was thinking at the time, even as he struggled to free his twin, that he couldn't remember the last time they had been so physically close to one another. Paul's seat had caught fire and the air in the car had become thicker. He had started to cough and choke, his eyes watering against the smoke. He tried to stay.

"It was too much," Sam said. He blinked away tears and now he couldn't even be sure if the boy was alive or dead or if Paul could hear him or not.

The boy gurgled and Sam wiped away the tears with the back of his hand. He gripped more tightly to the boy, hanging on to the sense that the boy was the bridge between himself and Paul.

The boy's lips moved.

Sam leaned close. He breathed in the stench of burning flesh and swallowed it down into his stomach.

"Your fault," he heard Paul say. And then the boy died.

CHAPTER THIRTY-FOUR

"Not your fault," Paul said, grasping the burnt child in desperation as the image of his brother faded from the dead boy's eyes. "I was as much to blame as you."

He gripped the boy's blackened arms more tightly, shaking him like a faulty telephone, but his fingers just sunk into the arms, like they were made of nothing but cinder. The flesh slewed off in great lumps and the bones underneath crumbled like chalk. The boy's left arm fell to the forest floor and was instantly lost upon the dark branches of the trees. The right hung by threads of melted tendons.

Paul felt François grab the back of his arms, pinching his skin painfully as he drew him back from the corpse. As he let his friend pull him into the middle of the forest path, the boy's head gave a sudden jolt like he still had some glimmer of life in him. Yet it was a false hope. His head slumped forwards, like a passenger nodding off on a long train journey. The boy's jaw disintegrated, causing his head to loll even lower, until the muscles in his neck snapped and his head fell off. With it the rest of his torso collapsed into his pelvis, falling to the ground in a cloud of black soot.

Cookie gasped. François gagged and Paul coughed as they retreated from the powdered remains of the boy. Only one hand and wrist were left, still nailed to the tree, like he was waving them farewell.

"Let's get the fuck outta here," Cookie urged. François nodded. Paul did not say anything. He followed after Cookie and François in a daze, his mind reeling after losing contact with his twin. They made for the left-hand fork in the path that

Cookie had explored earlier. The decision on which way to go was forgotten now. The urgency to get moving away from the boy's ashes was paramount.

"Was that your bro?" Cookie asked after they had walked in silence for what had seemed about fifteen minutes.

"Yes." Paul managed only a choked whisper. All he could think about was the quest to find Sam. Wracking his brains to remember if he had said anything useful on the direction they should go to find him. Or trying—unsuccessfully—not to dwell on the eerie way they had found to communicate after all these years apart. They walked on in silence again. Paul could not shake the smell of the burnt boy from his nose. It reminded him of that night, of the smell of his own flesh cooking, the pain of his palms melting on the burning car window.

He went to wipe his nose with his hands, but saw they were covered with the sooty remains of that poor unfortunate boy. He wondered who he was and what connection he could have with his brother.

Cookie led the way, with a nervous-looking François at her left side eyeing up the corpse trees. Paul was looking at the back of Cookie's skates as she rolled along the dark path. He noticed the path was inclining as they went on. It was gradual at first, but soon he began to feel it in the tightening of his ankle muscles.

Paul looked up to see the path was at a steeper gradient now. The upside-down burnt trees were peeling back before them, away from the path edge. The corpses were nailed to one tree in two. Then one tree in three and then four, before there were no more left. As the burnt dead bodies faded, they were also leaving the darkness behind them as well. All three of them exchanged mute glances as the orange glow before them increased.

Paul and his two companions looked left and right. The trees seemed repelled by the increasing glow. Their dim outlines could still be seen far off on each side of the path, but the light seemed to be blinding them out of existence.

Soon on the steep path there was nothing but the oblong orange glow ahead, like a door in the heavens. Cookie was finding it hard going in her roller skates, so she accepted a shoulder from each of the boys to help her along. The dazzling orange oblong above the end of the path grew closer with every hard step until they finally made it underneath its radiance. There seemed to be vague outlines of the orange-bleached stones and bricks on the corners beneath it. They were all suspicious of the thing above them, but so very glad to be free of the dark forest of corpses at last.

"Any chance of a bunk-up, guys?" Cookie said with a smirk to her male companions. François smiled back at her, but did not get the joke, while Paul just shook his head and offered his interlocked hands. François steadied her as she put her arm on Paul's shoulders and pushed up into the rectangle of bright light. Her head, arms, and chest vanished from sight for a few seconds, then she pulled herself down again to talk to them. "It don't look like much, but it sure beats the hell outta this shithole. Push me up again."

The boys did as they were told. She disappeared totally from sight, then her left arm reached down through the oblong of orange light. François grabbed it and Paul helped him up. Paul was alone for two seconds before François's and Cookie's hands dipped through the light for him. He took a standing jump and caught their hands in his. With a little effort they pulled him up through the light into the bottom of a grave.

CHAPTER THIRTY-FIVE

Sam felt as if he'd been hit with a sledgehammer. Your fault—he had heard it from Paul directly now. It was no longer just his own belief that his brother blamed him for the accident, now he knew it.

He collapsed onto the ground next to the dead boy. He sat on the hard pan, the stench of burning flesh still strong in his nostrils. It took all his willpower not to scream out the anguish that overwhelmed him. There was no way he could continue living like this, not with this burden of guilt. His first instinct was that he needed to finish it, but he'd tried that. He'd taken the step off the chair in the belief that it would be the end of his torment and instead it had simply brought him to a place in which he was at once closer to Paul and yet still so very, very far away from him.

"Don't give in now," he muttered to himself. "You betrayed Paul once before and you're not going to do it again." There was gravel in his voice—a steeliness that he did not even recognise in himself. He looked at the charred husk of the boy next to him. *I didn't even know his name.*

Maybe the boy had found the answer. Maybe the boy was now sitting in some paradise where he would spend his eternity. Maybe, but it didn't feel right to Sam. It wasn't just the obvious agony he'd had to go through, it was something more profound. What was that trite saying his mum used to trot out—two wrongs don't make a right? It was impossible for Sam to believe that the way a suicide could escape their punishment was by making the same mistake again. No, the boy was gone. He didn't know where, but wherever his soul was—if indeed that was what this was all about—it was not likely to be in a better place. Sam shuddered at the concept of a hell even worse than the one in which he found himself.

He stood up slowly, on legs that felt as weak as straw. He paused for a moment over the black corpse and wondered whether he was supposed to bury the boy, and in turn that thought made him wonder whether he was being watched, judged. Maybe the Great Creator was staring at him at this very moment, deciding whether or not he had suffered enough.

Sam shivered. The very idea of it gave him the creeps. He much preferred the idea that there was no final judgement, no reckoning of all the right and wrongs in his life. Maybe that was just because if he took an objective tally of his own life, he already knew which way the hammer would fall.

And yet he was here, in this hinterland of the dead. Surely that had to prove something. This place was a statement that life was a lot more complicated than he had ever believed.

Giving up wasn't an option. He'd tried that already. Giving up would just take him further away from Paul.

He didn't think about what would happen the next time they met—face to face rather than through the conduit of a burning child. He couldn't think about that, because if he did, then the guilt would overwhelm him. He had to focus on the positive: Paul was out there somewhere.

Sam looked around him. Back in the direction from which he had come was the grand sweep of headstones of the old graveyard, nubs of granite and marble jutting up from the earth like crooked teeth. At this distance the wall looked like a pitiful object. He considered walking back and trying to climb it once again—it was the only positive act he could think of—and yet the idea of spending his eternity trying and failing to climb that wall felt like a particular type of cruelty. He wasn't sure he wanted to believe in a God who would come up with that punishment, even if he deserved it.

The boy was gone. The boy who had guided him through this place. The old woman and the man were lost somewhere back there, too. He was alone.

He understood the attraction of the cult. He could join them now, but what had the boy said—that it was a false hope? He imagined himself as part of that huge mob of people scouring the ground, searching for a way out of this place, finding nothing and gradually becoming more and more embedded in the group until he would lose his sense of self. He would walk around this place and forget why he was trying to get out.

What he needed was God—the Great Creator, the boy had called him—to show him the way. He thought about joining his hands together and raising his eyes up to the sky and pleading to be given a sign. Any sign.

"Please?" he asked.

Sam looked around and laughed aloud to himself when he realised he was half expecting to see a big comedy hand with a pointed finger indicating the way he had to go.

"It's not going to happen. If you want to get out of here, you're going to have to find your own way," Sam told himself.

He shrugged. That was okay. He felt comfortable with the idea that he had to fight to get back to Paul. At least he now knew for certain that Paul was out there. Before he had felt it, but now he knew, and that meant it didn't matter if it took ten weeks or ten years or ten millennia, they were going to get back together.

He turned a full circle in the sand, peering out to the horizon and trying to decide which direction he should take. His initial instinct was that it didn't actually matter which way he went, all were equally pointless.

There were no comedy hands. There was no blazing insight that showed him the path he needed to follow. There was just the flat ground and the sky bleeding into the horizon.

He started to walk. Away from the dead boy. Away from the man and the old woman. Away from the cult. Away from the graves with their pits yawning open to spew out the newly dead. Away from the wall. Away from everything he knew or thought he knew.

Into the unknown. The welcoming unknown.

CHAPTER THIRTY-SIX

The first thing Paul noticed when François and Cookie pulled him from the shallow grave was the wall.

It dominated the whole left side of the vista, running up to a hill with a small chapel on top. The other side did not seem that far away, nor the wall too tall to climb. He moved past François to stand on the tomb and brushed his fingers together to remove the clay-coloured grave soil from his hands. Then he raised his left hand to shield his eyes as he panned around the new vast graveyard. The sun was low in the sky, like it was almost dusk, casting an orangey glow across the necropolis.

Paul pulled at his nostrils for comfort and gazed over the wall. He squinted against the harsh, low orange sunlight. He blinked several times and thought he could make out the faint tinges of grey-blue.

"Is this it? Are we here?" Paul asked Cookie, who François was helping up onto the tomb he stood upon.

Cookie licked her finger and raised it in the air. There was no wind and it seemed warmer than any other plane or place they had ventured through. She patted Paul hard on the back and smiled thinly. "I think we are."

"In the afterlife of Suicides?" François asked, stepping up next to Cookie, so they stood in a row.

"Yes, honey," Cookie nodded with a wide smile. Then her face took on a more serious look. "We must be extremely careful, boys, this is one of the Great Cremator's realms."

François looked around anxiously. "Then we better start looking for Paul's brother."

"Best idea I've heard since I died," Paul said cheerfully. He wasn't afraid; he had a calm sense that his brother was on this plane somewhere.

"Where do we start looking?" François opened his arms wide, his open palms cast red by the setting sun.

François had spoken what Paul had been thinking. This place looked as vast as his own afterlife, so he tried to put himself in his brother's shoes. He closed his eyes and breathed in slowly, then opened them and exhaled, his eyes darting from the bottom of the grave to the wall. "If I ended up here alone, the first thing I would do would be to try and scale that wall."

"Good call, sugar." Cookie pointed in that direction. "Let's move, shall we."

François shrugged and jumped down off the tomb. He turned and raised his arms to help his lover down. Cookie giggled a little in his arms and they kissed briefly. Feeling like a gooseberry, Paul jumped down to lead the way over to the wall. It took longer than expected, but he had got used to that by now. Things always seemed closer than they really were in these places.

This was death, Paul had to constantly remind himself, not life—the rules were different here. It hadn't mattered in the Afterlife of Accidents; he had gotten used to the way the place did or didn't work. Yet since his quest to find his twin brother had begun, he had learnt not to take things he saw at face value. These afterlife planes had only one thing in common: they were unpredictable.

It felt like it took almost an hour to reach the wall, but he could not be sure. Yet as they had neared their destination, the wall seemed to grow in height. It was so extreme right next to the old stone wall that you could see the top move up and down, if you rocked back and forth.

"He would not be able to climb this, mon ami," François said. He looked up and gave a long, exhaled whistle.

"No, but he would have tried," Paul said, hands on his hips, looking up at the top of the wall. It was so high it hurt his neck to crane up to see it.

"And he would have failed," Cookie said abruptly. "So what would your twin do then?"

Paul's left cheek twitched with anger at Cookie's words. He forced his muscles to relax. She was right, of course. Paul pulled at his nose again. He looked left and then right up the slope of the vast cemetery to where the sun blurred his vision to tears.

"If I failed at this, I think I would have headed off towards the setting sun, up that hill there."

There were two tall posts stuck in the ground halfway up the hill, with two planks of long timber fixed as crossbeams. There were human skulls attached to the top of each pole. Apart from that, it reminded Paul of some Western desert graveyard from the cowboy films he watched as a boy.

Paul pointed towards the crossbeams and the rising hill beyond. The unmoving low summer sun made staring at that direction for any amount of time hard on the eyes.

"Good a place to start as any, hun," Cookie said raising her hands to cup over her long eyelashes so she could see better.

"But not the right way," said an old female American-accented voice from behind them.

They spun around to face the stranger behind them, only Cookie on her roller skates doing it with any style. A short, thin, ancient-looking woman, with a ruddy-lined face stood before them.

"I beg your pardon?" Paul said politely.

"I said if you are looking for your brother Sam, you are looking in the wrong direction."

Paul exchanged guarded glances with his companions. "Where is he?" he asked.

"I'll take you to him," she said, and then smiled a near-toothless grin. "For a price."

CHAPTER THIRTY-SEVEN

The world ahead of Sam was lost in a heat haze. The red sun dripped from the sky and spilled over the horizon like hot treacle. It was impossible to know where the land finished and the sky began, and as Sam walked he realised that he was afraid that somewhere ahead of him there was no land or sky, there was just this single melted nothingness.

He trudged forward, dragging one foot after the other. The sun gouged the sight from his eyes and pricked the back of his neck with its heat. He closed his eyes, but it made little difference because the bright sunshine pierced his thin eyelids and scratched into his skull. Part of him wanted to lie down in the dry dirt and cry or scream at the unfairness. Part of him wanted to give up. The only thing keeping him walking was that Paul was out there.

So he walked. He pushed his body beyond anything reasonable. Sweat ran down the side of his face and it felt like he was standing in front of the burning boy once more. No, not in front—he was standing *inside* the burning boy. He *was* the burning boy. The thought did not frighten him as it might have done when he had first been hauled out of the grave into this strange land. In a short time he had become accustomed to this place. When he raised his hand to his forehead to wipe away the sweat and it came away stained with his blood, he shrugged and carried on walking. Because whatever plans the Great Creator had for him, he didn't think he was going to be allowed to walk himself to death.

He realised he was grimacing. His lips were locked in a tight grin. He could feel the muscles in his face ache and he wondered how he would look to anyone who approached him.

"Sam!"

He stopped. He cocked his head to one side in the hope that this would help him hear better. At first all he could hear was the sound of his own heart thumping in his chest. But there was something else. Something out there. His name. He was sure he'd heard someone whisper his name.

Into the rushing silence came a thousand simple noises: the whisper of sand pushed by the wind, the creak of a dead branch on a dead tree. He thought he heard the engine of a car somewhere way, way off in the distance, but that had to be his imagination because it sounded just like the car he and Paul used to drive.

He listened. And he waited. He heard voices so soft they were the touch of silk upon cotton. Barely even a breath on the air. Words. His name.

He started to run forward. Understanding fell upon him and suddenly he knew. It wasn't some slow revelation, it was immediate and it was complete. He knew! He knew!

This was what people experienced when they found God. It was a knowledge that came to him so perfectly that there was no way to question it. He understood in the same way he understood that to put one foot in front of the other was to walk, or to take one breath after another was to breathe.

He knew.

The Great Creator was calling him home.

His legs struggled to keep up with the need to run forward and he almost fell, except now the Great Creator held him in his gentle arms, and when Sam overbalanced he remained upright.

Nothing can hurt me now, Sam thought.

He cupped his hand over his brow and looked across the desert. The only change in the landscape was his blurred footprints scratched into the ground. He stared at the footprints for a moment, thinking that they were the only thing that proved he existed. As he watched, his footprints disappeared as if an invisible broom had swept across the desert floor and removed every trace that he had ever stood there.

Sam took a single step forward and checked behind him.

On the spot where he had stood, the ground held the slight indentation of his footprints, but even as he watched they faded away.

Panic rose within him. *The Great Creator will protect me,* Sam thought, but the confidence slipped away from him. What had the Great Creator done for the boy? The Great Creator was not calling him. The Great Creator had forgotten that this place even existed.

Which meant that the voice he heard calling his name and urging him forward was not trying to help him.

Fear shredded his soul. An overwhelming terror. Sam ran forward and then looked behind him and there was no trace of his passage across the sand. It was like he no longer existed, like everything he had experienced since waking in the coffin was a lie.

He stopped running, paralysed by the sense that instead of running away from danger he might be running toward it. Now he understood why rabbits stood quivering in the middle of a road when they saw the headlights of a car: because it was impossible to make a decision.

That was him: a rabbit crushed between the oppressive sky and the flat land around him.

The image rang true. Too true. It was how he had acted after Paul had left him. He had wasted the remaining years of his life waiting for something to happen. Waiting for a tap on the shoulder to tell him what he should be doing and where he should be going, and when that tap had not happened, he had burrowed down and down into nothingness.

"No!" he tried to shout out the denial, but it escaped from his lips as a whisper, as if he were afraid of being overheard, even in this empty place.

"No," he tried again. His voice cracked under the word. Just a single word and yet it felt so difficult to say aloud.

Shouting his dissent into the sky made a difference. "I will find Paul," he said. "I will not give up on him again."

He started to run across the flat lands. He looked behind him at the untouched ground and he laughed. He wasn't sure why it was so funny, but he couldn't stop himself and tears were streaming down his cheeks. He laughed and he ran and didn't stop even when the pain felt like someone had stuck a blade into his chest and twisted it to gouge out his lungs and his heart. He laughed and he ran. Ran and laughed. And laughed.

Until he reached the chapel.

CHAPTER THIRTY-EIGHT

"You look like his son," the old woman said in Paul's direction, before walking off towards the raised line of tombstones.

Paul raised his eyebrows and gave a shoulder shrug to his companions. "Hey, wait, we haven't said we believe you yet."

"But you will still follow me," she said, walking briskly away from the stagnant trio. Paul looked at his friends for guidance.

"Anything is better than staying round here, sugar," Cookie said helpfully.

Paul's eye darted to where François was perched on a tomb, giving his standard, bored-looking expression.

"Oh, you want my opinion, eh?" The Frenchman gave a little laugh. "We've made far worse decisions since we started this little quest. What are we waiting for?" François hopped off the tomb, then held his hand out for Cookie to take.

"Why thank you kindly, sir," she said mimicking a Southern Belle accent.

"Come on then," François urged, "before the old lady is lost from sight."

Paul frowned, turning to look at where he reckoned the old woman should have reached by now. She was much farther away than he imagined. He hurried after her, with his friends in tow. This was the right place to find his brother, he knew that. It was just a matter of finding him in this vast, spaced-out graveyard. He ran to catch up, with Cookie and François doing their best to do the same. It took five minutes before they were close enough behind the old woman to slow down a little and catch their breaths.

The woman led them through the tombs and wooden markers. On and on they trudged, until the graves became more intermittent. Finally, they left every single grave behind and entered a flatland where there was nothing to see, except her figure was always just ahead of them.

"Madame … madame?" François hurried to close the ever-constant gap between them and their spritely older guide. She did not stop to answer him. The old woman did not turn her shawl-covered head. She hadn't spoken since she led them from the tombstones into the rubble of dusty orange stones and beyond the markers of the graveyard. They had followed her away from the wall, over sand dunes, and into dustbowls. "Look, you stupid old hag of a shrivelled-up prune. My English friend here is too polite and too desperate, I fear, to annoy you like this, but I am not. Where in God's Heavens are you fucking leading us, you deaf, rancid-smelling bag of old putrid bones?" François turned to Cookie—who was following behind him next to Paul—and gave her his most broad, winning smile.

Cookie just groaned and looked down at her socks. Her roller skates were strung around her neck, as it was easier on her feet as they walked through deep red sand. Paul said nothing. He just followed after the old crone, like she was leading him to the *Promised Land*.

Getting less than feeble replies from his two companions, François returned his attention to the back of the old woman. She seemed to have jumped ahead five metres in the two seconds he had taken to look back at Cookie. "Mon dieu, this cannot be."

Shaking his head, he began pumping his arms as he ran as fast as the sand beneath his old shoes would allow. François gritted his teeth, making a growling sound deep in his throat. The world ahead of the old woman seemed to shimmer like low fog on a glass-still lake. He could see the curvature of the Earth as he concentrated all his effort on catching up to the woman. The very edges of his vision seemed to darken like he was running into a tunnel. All his efforts were fixed upon the ragged clothes that hung off her back. He could vaguely hear both Paul and Cookie faintly calling his name behind him. Yet he knew if he turned around and lost concentration on his task, the old woman would somehow leap forward in the blink of an eye.

They crested the top of a tall dune. He could no longer hear his friends' voices, only the rushing of blood in his ears. With one last effort of will, strength, and energy he grew close enough to try and grab the old woman's shoulder. His flailing right hand grabbed hold of her shawl. It slipped backwards to reveal nothing but a white sun-bleached skull. It had no skin attached and was dotted with intermittent wisps of pure-white hairs.

In an instant the skeletal remains of the old woman fell to the sand in a heap, covered by her grey rags. François overbalanced forwards and lost his footing on the sand dune's summit. The first he knew he was falling was when sand entered his screaming mouth. The orange sky and red sand switched from sky to ground in a merry dance as he tumbled down the other side of the dune.

Finally, he came to a gasping, coughing stop, covered with sand. Dazed and very confused, he stared up at the crest of the dune. He could see no sign of the woman's remains, only his two friends staring down at something high above on the top of the dune from whence he fell.

He was still spitting out gritty, hard sand when his two companions, who took a more sedate and careful route down, joined him. "So is she a bag of old bones still?"

Paul and Cookie did not answer. They were just staring past him, the opposite way to which he sat. Emptying his left shoe of sand, he turned round to see what had grabbed their attention. The sand from his shoe ran out as he stared at a small, simple, slate-grey stone chapel no more than three hundred feet from where he sat.

CHAPTER THIRTY-NINE

Sam did not move forward. He knew that he'd been staring down at his shoes rather than watching where he was headed, but still this made no difference. The chapel was there, in front of him, where he was sure that minutes earlier there had been nothing. It was a trick. A mirage. He'd watched enough Westerns to know that in the desert the heat and thirst had a way of preying on a person's mind and causing them to see things which did not really exist.

But it looked real. It looked really fucking real.

I know this place, he thought. He stood a good distance away and stared at the chapel. It was a small building, definitely a chapel rather than a full-blown church. A simple structure—a door with heavy-leaded windows, a sloping roof, and a crooked crucifix at the pinnacle. It was built from rough, grey stone—huge slabs that looked like they had just been pulled whole from a mountain somewhere in Wales and dragged to this place for the sole purpose of creating the building.

It's a long way to come to listen to a service, he thought. He took a step forward and watched the window on the left of the door. Had he seen something move? The flicker of a shadow passing across the glass? He shook his head and dismissed it as his imagination, or maybe the reflection of a cloud passing in front of the sun, but then he looked up and the sky was cloudless and the sun burned down on him uninterrupted.

It felt cold. Sweat rose on his brow and the back of his neck and he tried to persuade himself that it was just a pocket of cool air out here in the desert. Just a pocket of cold air. It wasn't that he was afraid. It wasn't that each moment he looked at the chapel his eyes itched and he had to fight the urge to scratch them out of his head so that he would no longer have to watch.

The chapel. The chapel. The words sang in his head, echoed like an almost-forgotten children's nursery rhyme.

I'm going to the chapel and I'm gonna get married.

He smiled at the snatch of music going around in his head and tried to remember the last time he had set foot inside a chapel. Then he remembered, and he didn't just feel cool, he felt cold. Cold as ice. Cold as death.

The last time he had been in a chapel—and now he recognised the building in front of him and he wondered how he could ever not have known what he was looking at—had been to plant his brother in the ground.

The shadow passed across the window on the other side of the door. Sam followed the movement with his head, snapping around but managing to just miss actually seeing the dark shape against the glass so that again all he got was the sense of someone moving around inside the building.

"Probably just some old priest," he said. The words were flat and lifeless. They butted against the cold air and the hard stone of the chapel and they dropped out of the sky like dead birds.

"Some old priest," he repeated to himself. He wanted to believe it was true. He wanted to believe it more than anything he could ever remember wanting in his life. More than wanting to lose his virginity to his brother's girlfriend, Trish. More than wanting to find Paul. More than wanting to save his own life. He stared hard at the window of the chapel and willed the shape on the other side of the glass to be something innocuous like an old priest mooching around in tatty old robes that flowed around his sandalled ankles.

Because the chapel was his way to Paul. He understood that. He didn't understand how he had come to find himself in this place. He was unable to draw a line from his brother's blood splashed across the cracked windscreen of the upturned car and the door of the chapel. He couldn't make sense of the journey, but he knew that the only chance he had of finding his brother lay behind the door. And whatever was inside there waiting for him…

A flicker of shadow crossed the window, as if taunting him to come inside. Daring him like a gang of kids on the edge of a school playground, out of sight of the teachers: *You do it. No, you do it.*

He closed his eyes and took a step forward. It seemed that he could feel the cold coming off the stones in waves and he smell the flat, grey building in front of him that stank of the grave. Not the grave from which he had risen, but a crypt in which a body had lain and desiccated until it was nothing more than old rags and powder.

He heard the sand crunching beneath his feet with each step he took. He tried to breathe, but it seemed to him that his chest grew tight from the lack of oxygen.

When he opened his eyes, he was standing directly in front of the building. Close enough to reach out and touch it with the flat of his hand.

The door was wooden. Old. Everything about the building was ancient. The wood had faded to pale grey, almost white, and Sam could see scratches on the surface where sand had scoured the wood.

There was a gnarled black iron handle. Sam reached out to take it and it felt like he was watching someone else move. Or maybe that he was watching someone else move him.

The metal was warm to the touch, and when he tried the handle, it turned easily.

CHAPTER FORTY

"I think I know that place," Paul said, pointing to the slate-grey chapel they slowly walked towards.

"What, from when you were alive?" François moved up to his left, dusting off as much sand as he could find, but there always seemed to be more.

"Not sure." Paul shook his head. "Maybe, from a dream."

"A dream you've had since dying?" Cookie, to the right of him, asked.

"Yeah, like being inside somewhere dark and then floating up from inside that place and it filled with friends and family, and Sam."

"Well, what are we waiting for, let us go there," François said, increasing his walking pace a little.

Paul though, stopped dead. He looked behind him. There should have been three sets of tracks leading back from where they walked, but there were none. It was sizzling hot and, standing still, he felt the heat even more. Paul felt a familiar icy chill creep up from his funeral-best shoes, up the back of his thighs to make his sphincter close tightly shut.

His friends had noticed he had stopped and turned together, equidistant ahead of him.

"What is it, Paul?" asked François, concern all over his features.

Paul couldn't answer. The freezing cold had wormed its way into his spinal cord. Flowing ever upwards towards the nape of his neck. He knew he had to move now or be paralysed on the spot any second.

"RUN!" He managed to turn his head to the side to look

backwards, before the cold fear shut him down.

Then he saw it.

They all saw it.

Out of the ochre sky it came, emerging from nothing, like it had been hidden behind an invisible cloud. It was vast, filling most of the eastern sky with its leviathan presence. Four Boaters drew it across the sky, hovering two hundred feet above the desert floor. It was monstrously dark in colour, hard lines of black, dark grey, and vivid red. The front of it reminded Paul of one of those cowcatchers on the front of an old American West train. From the spiked ends hung the burnt remains of at least fifty corpses. Its underbelly was lined with row upon row of dark grey chains and at every link there was a dead man, woman, or child. Its immense size vibrated the arid desert air around it, only interrupted by the faraway scream of another lost soul. It moved through the air, dripping blood from the uncounted corpses strung around its belly, leaving in its wake a red road across the desert sky.

A vast grey wheel was fixed in the centre of the platform. Upon it rested a blackened skull. It was nestled on a mound of white bones. Rivers of livid red blood poured from the gaps between the ivory teeth of its dark mouth. The blood ran down the deep grooves, towards the vast wheel, powering it. Its black sockets belched fire, sending soot into the air, joining the smoky air that clung around it like a dark fog.

Slowly the leviathan moved closer, darkening the desert behind them into night.

Paul felt someone grab his arm and spin him around. If he had been on his own, he was sure he would not been able to turn his gaze away from the monstrous floating machine of death. François punched his other arm for good measure, and they turned and fled once more across the desert. There was nothing but the grey chapel ahead of them. Paul wasn't sure the place could be much of a refuge, but it was all they had.

The chapel had seemed much closer at the bottom of the dune, but now it seemed miles away. Fear had sapped his energy levels and he ran on tired legs. They seemed to increase in weight with every footfall on the hot desert sand. It felt like he had just stepped out of a swimming pool after a long swim.

He glanced back to see that the shadow from the deathly machine was now racing across the orange sand behind them. Both his companions were struggling, too. The chapel was closer now, but the shadow was catching them.

A muffled cry and then a scream told him something was wrong before he saw it. The darkness had caught up with Cookie. A barbed spear on the end of a long black chain had pierced through her left breast. He and François turned to see the instant of fear in her eyes, before she was hauled up into the dark underbelly of the beast.

"Noooooo," François cried, his hand grabbing for the thin air where Cookie had stood. She was propelled up into the dark shadows and lost from view.

François stopped, tears rolling down his face. Paul saw the darkness cover his friend and charged into it to knock François down just in time, as a barbed spear on the end of another chain penetrated four feet deep into the desert floor, where François had just been standing.

"The Chapel," Paul urged, pulling his friend to his feet.

Another chain shot down. It pierced poor François through the belly and hauled him away into the hovering darkness. Paul felt his friend's hand wrenched from his grip and then he was gone. Paul could do nothing but turn and run. The chapel was so near now. He ran on with fear powering his aching muscles, but still the darkness overtook him, four feet from the open chapel door. He jinked right as the spear chain grazed past his left leg and he dived for the open chapel doorway.

CHAPTER FORTY-ONE

Sam pressed down on the handle. It moved silently. For a moment he was frozen by a terror he could not understand. When he heard the catch of the door release, it was like someone had poured ice into his soul.

From somewhere a million miles away, in a different universe, he heard the mournful wail of a train whistle. The sound was so pale it was almost non-existent, but in the stillness of the desert it carried to him. There was something romantic about the sound—it made him think about wide-open prairies with cattle and bison roaming free through golden fields of wheat that stretched to the horizon. He smiled, Paul had always wanted to go to America—it was one of those things they'd talked about as kids. He could imagine Paul now, sitting back on his horse with his wide cowboy hat shading his eyes from the blazing sun. He would have liked that. That would be his own kind of heaven.

Sam smiled at the image. They would be together again soon, he was sure of it. Not in this hell but in a better world. Maybe Paul's heaven. Sam accepted that he didn't deserve it, not after everything he had done, but he was confident that the Great Creator was a forgiving god.

He pushed open the door to the chapel.

The air tasted of dust. It felt like he was the first person to have entered the building in a decade, maybe a century. "Hello?" His voice was flat in the stillness of the building and he imagined the sound drifting through the empty chapel without finding an ear. It was hard not to be disappointed. Even though he wasn't sure what he was expecting, it was more than this, more than nothing. It would have been too much to expect to find Paul sitting inside waiting for him to arrive, and yet he accepted that this was exactly what some part of him had expected.

The door opened into a foyer. Wooden panels walled the inside of the chapel. It took Sam a moment to realise what was wrong—there were no windows and yet a grey light with no obvious source diffused through the air.

Before the door closed behind him, he heard the whistle of the train once more. He paused. It was louder this time. Closer. For a reason he could not explain, the idea of the train rushing towards him was no longer the comforting image that it had been. Now the scene in his imagination warped, only slightly at first so that initially it still appeared to represent the rural idyll of Paul on his steed as he watched the train race by, but as the train got closer it was apparent that the cowcatcher at the front of the train had been put into use. A single figure lay mangled between the metal tines of the grid. At first Sam assumed a steer or a bison had stepped onto the track and been swept up in front of the rushing train. But then it got closer. It was the boy. The boy trapped on the front of the train with a spear pierced through his chest and another through his neck and the black metal was rinsed with sticky red blood.

As the death train got closer, it skipped the tracks and started to plough through the field, pushing a growing mound of dirt in front of it. The mound became a hill, and from the heart of this soil—grave dirt, Sam thought as soon as he saw it—toppled bodies. Bodies of the freshly dead and those decades in the ground—nothing more than bones that stretched and snapped under the trauma. The dead boiled. Bones snapped. Skin burst open to eject congealed blood and shrunken lumps that were once vital organs: heart, liver, brain.

"Paul!" Sam screamed as the train charged toward his brother. His twin.

Paul…

The single word faded, as if a taunt.

Paul…

The door shut with a heavy thud and the vision fled, leaving

Sam alone in the dry silence of the wood-lined chapel with the memory of his cry trapped in his throat. The chapel door was solid. It was the sort of door that, once closed, would be difficult to open again.

He tried. Because now Sam knew that he had been tricked. By the chapel. By the Great Creator, or perhaps the other one… the Great Cremator? Maybe just by his own need to believe that Paul was close.

He was sure that Paul was not in the chapel with him. Paul was still somewhere out there. He didn't know where, but he was certain that he needed to be outside, looking for Paul, ready to help his twin when the time came.

Because the time was coming, Sam was sure of that. It was a knowledge that came from somewhere deep inside himself. A hidden knowledge that blossomed within him.

The door to the chapel had no handle. Not on the inside.

Sam rushed across. It wasn't possible. He remembered the handle that he had grasped on the outside of the door, he could almost feel the cool metal against the palm of his hand, and he remembered the silent way the handle turned and the door opened and admitted him into this sanctuary.

The space between the side of the door and the door frame was a pencil-thin slit, not even wide enough for him to insert his fingernails. He pawed at the door and in the still silence of the chapel he heard his own urgent, panicked breaths returned to him from the flat surface of the door. He sounded like an animal.

"Paul…" he whimpered.

His echoed voice taunted him. Mocked him.

He balled his hand into a fist and thumped the door, but it only had the effect of sending tremors up his arm and into his bones.

He slumped to the ground and a rogue voice inside his head—a voice that Sam refused to accept was really part of him—slyly pointed out that he had given up. Again.

Just like last time. He had stood at Paul's graveside in the rain, watching the vicar throw handfuls of dirt onto the lid of his coffin, and he had given up. A situation that had not changed until the moment when he had finally made a decision and stepped onto the chair with the ragged noose in his hand.

"Paul," he whispered.

Paul's gone, the voice inside him taunted. *Paul's gone and you will never see him again, however long you travel through this land.*

Sam started to scream, which was why he didn't hear the others approach him, not until they were in the chapel with him.

CHAPTER FORTY-TWO

Paul experienced pain like he had never felt since he had died. Tears ran down his cheeks, drawing muddy lines in the sand and dust that covered his pale face. He turned over on his back, causing aches to shoot up his elbows and knees from where he had grazed them jumping through the chapel doorway. Cool hard flagstones lay underneath his body as he pushed himself up into a sitting position. He was shaking from head to foot, sobbing and crying out for his lost friends. He hadn't felt pain like this since his untimely death. No one should, death dulled such things.

Paul stared out of the open doorway. The brightness of the sand was quickly extinguished by the shadow of the floating leviathan that had taken his companions. The red sand and sunlight were consumed and storm shadows plunged the outside of the chapel into utter darkness.

Paul winced as he stood up, confused by the pain he was feeling and the utter grief of his loss. He moved closer to the stone doorway, his left hand on the edge of the thick oak door. He tried to peer up and see where his friends had been taken, but could see nothing but a mass of writhing, charred bodies chained under the floating vehicle. Something blurred down at him at rapid speed, causing him to fall backwards in fright. A vicious barbed harpoon stopped only three inches from his nose. It hovered in mid-air for a second or two, before shooting back into the underside of the thing that hung over the chapel.

Paul let out a breath and then a nervous twitch of a laugh. The chapel was a sanctuary. Yet the discovery did nothing to lift the weight of loss that bore down on his shoulders. His friends and travel companions were up there! Outside, suffering who knows what kind of inhuman torments. If he stepped across the threshold, he would suffer the same fate.

He turned away from the doorway. Walking two steps to the place where he had landed, he took in his surroundings for the first time. He was in some octagonal antechamber, with a wooden door in each wall. Torches flicked in their sconces above each doorway. Above his head ran a panelled wooden roof pointed with naked rafters.

There were layers of dust everywhere, like it had been undisturbed for centuries. In the centre of the chapel there was a black iron cover over a stone font. The octagonal shade had slits in it. It was fixed to the stone pedestal with thick black bolts. He moved closer and tried to peer inside.

There seemed to be something glowing red. He pushed up on tiptoes to get a better angle but could not see the source of the illumination. He put his hands on the cover to lift it but flinched as it burnt his palms. He looked down at his hands and saw his skin was turning red. Pain flowed up his arms into his brain, crying out to be noticed.

"I've burnt my hands," he said to no-one. He'd never experienced anything like this in the afterlife. What was this place?

He exhaled and stepped away from the pedestal. He blew on his smarting palms and moved over to the door nearest the one through which he had entered. The chapel looked small when they had approached it and he wasn't sure how there could be seven other doors leading off in varying directions. He blew on his burnt right hand again and turned the thickly painted black ring to open the latch. He pulled it inwards only an inch when he heard a sound behind him. One of the black bolts shot out of the stone pedestal and hit the wall next to him.

Paul let go of the door handle, as it hurt to put pressure on his burnt skin. A second bolt was expelled from the font, and then a third and fourth, until all the bolts were exploded and the black cover of the eight-sided stone structure slowly ascended to the ceiling. Whatever levitated it, Paul could not see. He had wanted to see inside it; now he wished he hadn't when what was hidden inside came into view. There were two babies, floating on a cushion of red light. They were twin boys, joined together by a single umbilical cord. But that was not the most unnatural and disturbing thing about these two infants. They had no skin. Their entire bodies were covered with unblinking lidless grey eyes. The eyes were all fixed on him, filled with some ungodly malice that even chilled the burns on Paul's hands.

Two mouths opened, showing tongues also covered with tiny eyes, and they began to wail and screech like they hadn't suckled in days. Fear of the unknown left Paul and he dove through the door he pulled open, hoping it could not be any worse than the eye-covered wailing babies. He slammed the door behind him. Shutting out the primal wail of the twins.

He turned to see what room he was in now and found out he was not alone.

CHAPTER FORTY-THREE

Sam fell silent. His scream ceased, as if someone had taken a pair of scissors to his throat.

He waited for the figures to react. A group of five shapes that looked familiar but he couldn't quite place them. They were only ten feet away and yet they were vague, like ghosts seen through a sheet. They did not stir and yet there was something feral about them. About the way they stood there watching him. He was prey. He was *their* prey.

The sensible thing to do would be to get up and run, Sam understood that. He reckoned they would be on him before he was able to get to his feet, but he had to at least make an attempt to escape. If he could surprise them … if he could get to the door before they reacted … there was just a chance that he could escape the chapel. Then it would be a straight race across the open desert. He didn't rate his chances—one in a hundred seemed like reasonable odds from where he was sitting—but at least he would die out in the open.

Yes, running was the sensible thing to do, but how many times had his teachers or the local priest or one of the cops pointed out to Sam that he and sensible weren't even passing acquaintances?

The figure on the far left of the group was shorter than the rest. It looked to be no more than a child. Sam wondered what sort of gang this was, that they were happy to recruit kids to go around and murder people, and on holy ground as well—no sense of fair play.

Sam tried to move and at first the muscles in his legs refused to respond. He grimaced and nearly gave up right then. This was a sign. He wasn't supposed to do anything, his body knew that, even if he was too stupid to accept it.

The muscles in his left leg twitched, a spasm that ran from his hip down to his foot. His ankle slapped against the floor like a dying fish. But it was movement, and he wasn't entirely sure that it had nothing to do with him.

He tried again. Now both feet moved. He pressed the palms of his hands against the cold ground to lever himself upward and was probably as shocked as the gang when he moved. It would be a lie to say he sprang to his feet, it was more of a drunken lurch, and when he was upright, his body swayed.

The one in the middle, the ringleader no doubt, was familiar. The shape of his body… Sam's mind screamed at him to get out of the place, but instead he stood there and peered through the shroud that hung between him and the group.

"Sam?"

Sam blinked. As soon as he heard the voice, he knew Paul was standing in front of him. The realisation hit him hard. How could he be so stupid not to recognise his own brother?

"Paul?"

"Sam, is that you?"

His brother stepped forward and Sam staggered to reach him. The pair met in the middle of the room.

"Is that really you?" Sam asked. He wanted to laugh. It felt like he would simply explode if he didn't find a way to vent this emotion. This was Paul. This was his brother. His twin. This was the moment he had been searching for since he had woken in an upside-down car with the broken wreckage of his brother hanging beside him.

"I'm sorry," he said. He heard his voice break. His vision blurred, and as quickly as he wiped the tears away, they were replaced by more. He grinned and fully expected Paul to tell him he was a baby—always had been; after all, he was the younger by precisely seven minutes.

His cheeks ached and he wondered what he looked like—some hamster packing nuts, no doubt. He didn't care. Nothing mattered now. Not even that he was dead. Stepping off the chair, climbing that wall, even watching the boy burn—it had all been worth it, just for this moment.

He lifted his hands, but he didn't know what he was supposed to do with them. Hug him? Slap him on the back? Shake hands? Nothing felt appropriate.

And still, underneath the joy, there was a seed of doubt. There was the recognition that even when he was standing this close to his brother, it didn't feel right. He tried to convince himself that emotion clouded his vision. He was overwhelmed, that was why Paul, his brother, didn't … feel like Paul, not properly. Not really.

"Paul. Is that…" he hesitated even to ask the question. "Is that you?"

Paul nodded. And grinned.

"Really you?" Sam asked.

He reached out and his brother flinched from the touch, jerking his shoulders backwards.

Sam's hand stayed in the air, hanging like a mannequin. He didn't know what to do and eventually he let his hand drift back to his side. It was Paul, he was sure of that now. But Paul would not have avoided the contact. He might have said something stupid to diffuse the atmosphere between them—maybe even told Sam what a prick he'd been for driving too fast and to look what that had done to them—but he wouldn't have ducked away.

"What's wrong?" Sam asked.

He felt the muscles in his chest tighten. It became more difficult to breathe. It was like someone had reached inside his body and squeezed.

"Paul?"

He noticed movement to his left. The child stepped forward, out of the mist and into perfect view.

Sam stared. Maybe he shouldn't have been surprised, because why should he allow himself to be surprised by anything in a world where he woke up in a coffin and now found himself standing face to face with his dead brother, and yet seeing the boy again was wrong. Just wrong.

"But you're dead," Sam said. "I saw you burn." He realised he was checking the boy's face for any signs of the fire that had consumed him. There was nothing.

The boy smiled. An ugly smile that suggested he knew more than Sam. Much more than Sam.

"And yet here I am," he said. One of the figures behind him shuffled but did not move forward, and yet now Sam understood who was standing there—the old woman. The other two figures were too indistinct to see properly, and Sam wasn't sure that even if he had a clear view of them, he would recognise them.

"Paul?" He turned to his brother. "What's happening?"

Sam watched his brother's mouth twitch as if he were trying to say something but was being stopped. For a second he had the image that his brother's lips had been sewn shut—maybe as part of the preparation for his burial—and now he was standing there trying to break the surgical twine that silenced him.

"You're scaring me," Sam confessed.

His brother opened his mouth. Black teeth rotted in his gums.

"Run," he screamed. "Run before He gets you."

CHAPTER FORTY-FOUR

There were six doors, plus the door he had come through. Three of the doorways were blocked by solid, flat stone walls. Across the room from him, the central doorway was wooden and closed. On either side of that were two open doorways. In them, standing on the thresholds, stood Cookie and François.

A smile of relief flowed across Paul's face, but faltered as he took two steps towards them. Both his friends looked blankly at him. Both showed no signs of the trauma the barbed harpoons must have done to them.

"How did you get away?" his voice echoed around the heptagonal room's grey stone walls.

"The Great Cremator let us go," Cookie said, sounding like she had taken some posh *Pygmalion* voice-coach lessons.

"He wants you to join the fold," François said, his accent gone, like the Frenchman had been erased. It still sounded like him, but not—all at the same time.

"What the hell has he done to you two?" Paul stepped into the centre of the room. He looked from left to right at his friends. It seemed to him that their essence had been hollowed out, leaving only their physical husks behind. Soulless. Their voices did not echo.

"You need to come with us," Cookie pleaded, but with the lack of colourful passion that usually made up her rich vocal tones.

"We need you, friend," François chipped in.

"I-I don't think I will, guys. Why don't you come with me?" Paul waved his arms, gesturing them to enter the room. "Come and hug it out with old Paulie."

"He is waiting for you in the room beyond," Cookie said without moving from the threshold of the arched open doorway in which she stood.

"What, the Great Cremator? Don't think so."

"No, not He. Your brother, Sam, waits on the other side. He is very eager to see you again, my friend."

"No-no-no." Paul wagged his finger at the Frenchman. "Don't you fucking dare. I'm not your friend, whatever you are. And don't ever use my family to get to me. It won't work. Give me back my friends and brother and I might consider just kicking your bony arse only half to death and back again." Anger matched the tears welling up in Paul's eyes. His friends were gone, replaced by soulless puppets, and he had no idea where his brother was. He had no guides, no companions, nothing but his fists and blind rage.

Paul spun around, looking around the rest of the room for anything to use as a weapon. There was nothing but the arched doorways and a mosaic on the floor. It was of a red and black serpent with a child's head. Then he looked down at his shoes. Hopping from one foot to the next he tugged each shoe off his feet.

"Give me back my friends!" he roared at Cookie and François.

"NO," the same voice echoed from both their open mouths at once. It was loud, mocking, and deep like the bottomless pits of hell. "THEY ARE MINE NOW, TO DO WITH AS I PLEASE. I WILL EAT THEIR SOULS AND BURN THEIR FLESH FOR A MILLION YEARS UNLESS YOU GIVE YOURSELF TO ME."

Paul staggered back from the voice. It seemed like a wall of sound buffeting him backwards. He turned to seek the door he had come through, but it was gone. Only a hard stone replica stood in its place, with no door handle to grab onto.

"IF YOU DON'T WANT SAM TO SUFFER THE ABSOLUTION OF HIS FINAL CREMATION, JOIN ME OF YOUR OWN FREE WILL, PAUL." The voice seemed slightly softer now, like someone had turned down the bass.

"You don't have my brother, do you?" Paul looked up from under his eyelids at the husks of his two friends.

"HE SITS AT MY LEFT HAND. SHALL I SLICE OFF A

LENGTH OF HIS SKIN TO PROVE IT TO YOU? HE IS MINE, AS YOU WILL SOON BE, READY TO BURN TOGETHER AGAIN."

"You can't kid a kidder and I can smell bullshit a mile away. And you really should take something for that throat of yours." Paul was spurred into action, throwing his left shoe at Cookie, and then his right at François. Each shoe found its mark, passing through the figure standing in the door and dissolving them into clouds of grey ash. The ash exploded, blocking the whole doorway, before solidifying into cold grey stone.

The voice was gone.

Paul hurried forwards and felt each stone-covered doorway in turn. They were solid and he had no way of breaking them down. Only the wooden door in the centre remained in the seven-sided room. He grabbed the handle and paused. Paul wondered if this was a trap, too. Part of the Great Cremator's elaborate ruse to get him through this door. His fake friends hadn't been that hard to look through. Was that *Old Deep Voice's* master plan? To get him through this door?

Paul looked around the rest of the room at the blocked-out doorways. It didn't seem like he had much choice anyway. He took a deep breath, turned the ornate round iron handle, and pulled open the door.

The archway beyond the wooden door was completely blocked by cold grey stone. Somewhere beyond the stone he thought he could hear the sound of deep, booming laughter.

CHAPTER FORTY-FIVE

"Paul?" Sam asked. "What's happening?"

"NOTHING."

Sam blinked. His brother's voice boomed across the room and bowled him over. "You want to take something for that throat," he said. He smiled, but there was no response from his brother.

"You told me to run."

"NO," his brother said.

Sam winced. "Tone it down a notch. Inside voices, remember?"

"No," his brother said. Quieter now, but there was still something wrong with him. It was like he was testing the voice, not quite sure how it worked. Which was insane, and yet Sam couldn't push away that feeling of wrongness.

"I said come," Paul said.

Sam shook his head, but those seven minutes between them made a big difference. Paul was always first to everything: first into school, first into the playground. When they were fourteen, it had been Paul who had first stolen the can of Carlsberg from the cupboard under the stairs and snapped it open to take the first gulp. It had been Paul who had lit up their cigarette and dragged the smoke deep into his lungs until he had coughed it out and handed over the smouldering tube. Always Paul first: Paul with the girlfriend when he hooked up with Trish. Paul with the first job. Standing there looking at his brother, Sam felt that he had spent his entire life following in the footsteps of his older brother. Just seven minutes, and yet it made all the difference.

He looked at Paul and tried to remember the last time he

had ever disobeyed his brother, and he couldn't. It occurred to him that maybe he couldn't remember because it had never happened. Paul had led and he had followed, right up to that night coming home from the pub when he had flipped the car.

Paul took a step toward him.

Sam could look at nothing but the black gaps where his brother's teeth should be. He thought he saw something moving in the dark of his mouth. A flash of pale white.

The maggot slipped between two rotten teeth and hung for a second on Paul's lip before falling to the ground.

Sam stared as it squirmed on the flagstone between them. He looked at Paul, sure his brother would make a joke of it. He said nothing.

And then he knew. Or accepted. This wasn't Paul. This couldn't be Paul. Whatever stood before him had never…

"That girl in Year Six—what was her name?"

"Hannah," Paul answered.

"What did Mum say the day you knocked my tooth out with a cricket ball?"

"She said I should knock the other one out to even it up."

Sam tried to think of something else. Someone no-one but he and Paul would know.

"Where did you keep your porn mags?"

"In the middle of all my football magazines."

"You're not Paul."

"Of course I am."

"Of course he is," the boy said.

Sam turned his attention away from this brother—or whatever it was that was trying to pretend to be his brother. The boy returned his gaze.

"How would you know?" Sam asked.

"Of course he is. Listen to him."

"You never met him. You don't know."

"I know him. We all know him."

There was something about the way the boy spoke that sent a shiver of fear the length of Sam's clichéd spine. *We all know him.* It brought to mind a quote from the Bible—from one of those interminable morning assemblies that they were made to sit through. *My name is Legion, for there are many of us.*

In turn, the quote dragged back the image of the mob flooding between the headstones of the cemetery. One mind ruling over them all. One motivation.

Was that all they were? Was that all any of this was? A single entity? What did that make the Great Creator?

Legion was the Devil, at least that was what Paul had explained to him when they had talked about it in bed that night with the lights out. Legion was the Devil and Jesus had cast him out into … what was it? Sam struggled to remember the rest of the story. It hadn't seemed important at the time. He could recall nothing except that they were some sort of animals—cows or sheep or maybe a flock of birds—and they had died. He remembered that part. In the dark of their room their voices had slipped back and forth through the night. Paul had described it as Jesus's Kick-Ass moment.

"Am I in hell?" he asked.

"Of course not," Paul said.

Sam took a step backwards. It wasn't the words—the words were right. Maybe not exactly what Paul would say but close enough that it didn't make a difference. It was the way he said them. Automatic. There was no warmth there, no thought. He spoke like a computer retrieving a piece of information and relaying it back to the user.

He should run. Probably the only honest words his brother had spoken since he arrived in the room was his warning. Everything else had been bullshit, and not even Paul Wright bullshit. Just … bullshit.

He dared to take his eyes off the thing pretending to be his brother and look behind him. The door was near. He tried to calculate how long it would take to turn the handle and get outside, and he tried not to think about what Legion might do to him if he tried to escape.

"COME WITH ME," Paul said again. He smiled, and although it wasn't quite right, wasn't quite how Paul would have smiled if he had really been there in the room, it was close. Close enough.

He held out his hand. On the exposed flesh above his wrist the faded blue ink of a girl's telephone number stained his skin and Sam smiled. How many times had he seen that? Paul had called them Kill Markings.

Sam breathed out. A long sigh that seemed to hold all the tiredness and despair and loneliness since the day he had woken up in a hospital bed and looked across to discover that the bed next to him was empty. Flat sheets. A crash cart standing idly next to the plywood cupboard with the empty vase on top and the door open to reveal the bare inside of the cabinet.

He was tired. Tired of being alone. Tired of fighting.

He looked at the Kill Markings on his brother's wrist and made a special effort not to read the faded number written there. He still saw it, even if his mind refused to believe that it existed.

Nothing was quite right, but it wasn't wrong enough to reject. He'd been searching too long. Ever since he'd stepped off the chair and felt the coarse rope pull taut around his throat. He had given up too much to let it go now on a hunch. On an instinct that something was wrong.

He reached out and folded his hand inside his brother's.

CHAPTER FORTY-SIX

Paul moved back to the stone archway that had once been the door through which he had entered the seven-sided room. He banged it with his fist from top to bottom. It was solid as anything he'd felt since dying. He tried the open wooden door again. Closing it and pulling it sharply open like he had once done as a boy trying to catch the fridge light going off and on. He tried counting to his age in his head and then opening it. Then counted to seven, but it still remained blocked.

Then he tried the archways his doppelgänger friends had been standing in: both felt as solid as rock. Paul exhaled and looked down at his socks. He wiggled his toes, feeling the cold, hard floor beneath his feet. Scratching an imaginary itch on his forehead, he moved over to the two solid archways that stood adjacent, to give them a tap. He rapped the left-hand one with his knuckles. It was solid as all the others. Then side-stepping to his right, he tapped the next blocked-up archway with his right hand.

As he did, he heard a click, followed by a rumbling vibration of stone upon stone. Paul spun round searching for the source of the noise. The stone obstruction behind the open wooden doorway had slid down, leaving a two-inch gap at the top. Paul hurried over. He had to stand on tiptoes to peer through the opening. He could make out the top half of a white-marbled room beyond. His view wasn't helped by the fact that the secret stone portal before him was at least a foot deep.

Eyeing the thick stone block suspiciously, he put his hands tentatively into the gap and tried to push the secret doorway downwards. It was an exercise in futility.

Paul looked around the room at the various arches and then walked back to the one he was tapping when the stone block moved. He tapped it again from top to bottom, side to side and edge to edge. The stone block in the doorway did not budge again. Paul wiggled his fingers and looked at the five remaining archways.

"Maybe I have to tap them in a certain order to open the doorway," he said aloud to himself. He looked at the five choices and weighed up which to try next. He dismissed the way he had entered the room and then the two his fake friends had been standing in. That only left the one to the right and one across from it. Paul decided to walk across the room and tap the wall there, once.

He gave a yelp of victory as the block shuddered, rumbled, and lowered another two inches. It was now at his eye-height and Paul hurried over to peer through. There was another smaller white-marble room much the shape as the one he was standing in. He counted the walls and came up with only six.

"Right," he said clicking his fingers. "Eight, seven, and now, in there, is a six-sided room."

He had a choice to make again. Which stone archway to tap next? He opted for the one between the entry archway and the first wall. One rap of his knuckles brought another rumble and lowering of the block. Six inches of gap now. Not enough to get his head or chest through yet. He needed to tap another blocked archway, but which one? He quickly decided on the archway through which he had entered this room.

It was his first mistake.

The stone block rumbled as usual, giving him hope before dashing it completely. It moved back up and shut, leaving him walled up in the seven-sided room again.

"Shitshitshit … shit," he cursed, making his way over to the first archway he had tapped. "Please work again," he said and tapped it. Once more the block moved down to reveal a two-inch gap. He ran over to the second and then third arches he had tapped before. He was now back where he'd started and had another choice to make. He decided on the one that the fake Cookie had been standing at and was rewarded with an eight-inch gap. Then he moved to the stone arch where the fake François had been. Now the gap was ten inches.

It seemed a large enough gap to get his body through. Pulling himself up on the wooden door, he put his sock-covered feet on the edge of the gap. If he was going through, he was going as fast as he was able, so he could land on his feet. Paul pushed himself through the tight gap. As soon as his head was clear, the stone block came hurtling upwards. It took a few of the hairs from the back of his head with it, but he was through, falling to his knees on the hard marble floor.

He stood up and looked around the hexagonal room. The stone block behind was painted black in contrast to the white marble. Five red painted doors ran around the rest of the six-sided room, numbered in roman numerals I-V. Paul looked around the walls and ceiling.

"This is another fine mess you've gotten me into, Sam," he muttered to himself. Then he looked down at the centre of the marble floor. There was another red painted hexagonal shape with the roman numeral IV etched on it. "Oh great, another fucking puzzle."

CHAPTER FORTY-SEVEN

Sam held his breath and waited for the world to come crashing down around him. When it didn't happen immediately, he allowed himself a grin of relief. He had been overreacting, he knew it. He felt his brother's rough hand folded inside his own. It felt weird—he couldn't remember the last time they'd held hands—probably when they were kids and their mum had sent them to the shop together, hands joined as they crossed the roads. He smiled at the memory, smiled, and felt the relief flood through his body that at last they were back together. Nothing else mattered.

"Just Sam and Paul against the world. As it always has been. As it always will be," he said.

His brother said nothing. Instead, he took the lead, directing them out of the antechamber and deeper into the chapel. He pushed through doors, bringing Sam through a mourning room laid out with cushioned chairs and discreetly placed boxes of paper tissues where families could wait to say goodbye to their loved ones. Sam glanced around the room but the gentle tug of his brother's hand on his own swept him into a stone corridor with glass windows that painted multi-coloured pictures onto the grey walls of the chapel.

"Where are you taking me?" Sam asked.

Paul muttered under his breath.

"What?"

They passed out of the corridor and into a room at the back of the chapel, a room Sam was confident the public was never supposed to see. The soft crimson furnishings were gone, replaced by hard wooden chairs and a functional desk and a steel grey filing cabinet. The carefully decorated windows were now plain glass and looked out onto a red-brick wall.

Sam followed.

There was a door at the far end of the room, a cheap plywood affair painted white and pock-marked with small holes and the tattered remains of strips of Sellotape. In places the wood had faded to a dirty cream colour that outlined A4 patches of brighter paint that Sam assumed represented where notices or posters had previously hung.

A sound rose from the other side of the door. When Sam first heard it, he thought that it was voices—a cacophony of people whispering angry words. As he neared the door, he reached a better understanding—not voices. The roar of fire.

Paul seized the metal handle of the door.

"Wait!" Sam said.

His brother did not turn round. "Trust me."

Sweat dripped from Sam's brow into his eyes and he used his free hand to wipe it away. "What's behind there?" he asked. His mind provided its own image: a vista of red and black flames roaring out from a furnace that peeled flesh from bodies and scorched white bone into grey ash. He remembered standing in the chapel when Paul had been cremated and watching the red velvet curtains judder together and then the creaking of the closing doors. He remembered the rumble of metal rollers drawing the coffin off the stand and into the furnace.

The thought came to him: *What if this is a dream, a nightmare? What if everything since the moment I woke up in the coffin has just been the last few seconds of my existence?*

He pushed the thought away. It all felt too real to be a nightmare. He could pinch himself, but that would prove nothing. Ultimately, all he could do was believe that whatever was happening to him was real—real as anything had ever been. And that behind that door was … what exactly? He wasn't sure, but whatever it was, he accepted that it terrified him.

"I can't," he said. "I can't just trust you. Not this time."

He waited for Paul to come roaring at him and remind him that all of this was his fault—the overturned car, the hanged man's dance. Everything that had happened to both of them for the last ten years had been down to him. He hung his head and waited for his brother to pour down a decade's worth of rage.

"You have to," Paul said. His voice was soft. "It's the only way."

He pushed open the door and the sound of the furnace exploded across the room. Scorched air rushed through the gap in the door and Sam tried to run, but the first breath he took burnt his lungs. It was like swallowing fire. His eyes watered. His vision melted. He put his hand up to his eyes to protect them but all he could smell was the stink of burning hair—his own.

"What have I done to you?" he tried to ask Paul, but the words burnt in the air before they were even uttered.

The sound of the roaring flames coming from inside the room was like a tidal wave of noise. It crashed over him, drowning him.

His lips were dry, what little moisture there had been on them evaporated immediately. He could feel his skin crack and shrivel as it felt like every drop of water inside his body was squeezed out.

Sam staggered backward. His hands flailed in front of him and struck the wall, burning his fingers on contact. The smell of his own burning flesh filled his nose and scorched the back of his throat.

His knees buckled underneath him, so he crawled. The black and white tiles of the old linoleum flooring bubbled under his touch.

I just want to die, he thought to himself. He even felt his legs drawing up into his chest as he settled into a foetal position. *Just want to lie here and die.*

"That's right," Paul said. His brother's voice came from somewhere above him. Around him. Below him. Came from every direction at the same time. "That's right. Give up. Give yourself to me now. Give yourself to the Great Cremator."

Sam lurched away from the door. The heat inside the room was so intense that he couldn't see. The sound of the flames too loud to hear anything but them and Paul's voice. He could taste only his own burning flesh. Feel only the burning plastic as it melted over his fingers.

"Paul. Help me," he whispered. The words scraped the lining of his throat as he spoke.

He hauled himself across the floor. Each inch of ground was hard-won. Each tile he crossed was a victory.

The floor beneath him changed and for a moment he was too shocked to understand. It was cool. When he lifted his hand, his palm no longer dripped with melted plastic. The air against his cheek was sharp as a blade.

He dared to look behind him. Paul waited in the heart of the furnace. There was no suggestion that he would chase him. For a moment, Sam allowed himself the false hope that he might escape. When he looked forward once more, the scene was tinged pink and he assumed the colour came from bloody tears. He used the back of his hand to wipe them away and a smudge of crimson smeared across his bright red skin.

He tried to stand but his legs were too weak to hold him. The best he could manage was a staggered lurch forwards before he returned to his knees.

He checked behind him. Paul was gone. The door to the furnace was closed. The room was wood panelled with a black and white linoleum floor. There were no scorch marks on the dark wood, no blisters on the tiles. Motes of grey dust were trapped in a pale-yellow beam of sunlight and Sam heard the low breathing of the building. In. Out. In. Out.

He dragged himself out of the room. Across the threshold. Into a corridor which he did not remember. There were stained-glass windows and small stone statuettes embedded into the brick walls.

Ahead of him stood Paul. But when he cleared the blood from his eyes, the corridor was empty and he was alone once more, with just the weight of the building pressing down upon him.

The hand which grasped his ankle, and started to drag him backwards across the floor, was hot.

CHAPTER FORTY-EIGHT

Paul edged around the hexagonal shape in the centre of the floor. He wasn't sure why, but it screamed trap to him.

"Trust your instincts, Paulie," he muttered to himself. He made for the door with I on it and examined it. There were no traps or wires that he could see, but that meant nothing in this nightmare of a chapel. He did the same to the other doors, but it didn't help at all. They were all red with large black rings to pull them open. Only the red six-sided shape on the floor was any different.

He patted down his funeral suit, searching for anything to toss into the centre of the room. He came up with nothing. He looked down at his socks and wiggled his toes. He didn't even have a shoe to throw anymore. Then as he looked down, he spotted something he could use. One of his jacket buttons was loose, hanging by two threads. He pulled it off, the cotton snapping with satisfying ease.

Paul knelt down and moved as close to the hexagonal red shape as he dared and tossed the button onto the VI in the centre. It fell through instantly with a jet of fire, leaving the smell of bad eggs in the room.

"Not that way then," he said, wrinkling his nose against the funk coming from below. "The number six and it heading downwards, were a bit of a clue." Paul sat on his knees and looked around at the other doors. "Now which one of you five bastards do I choose then?"

"Well, my lucky number is three," he mused, wondering why he was speaking aloud to himself. Maybe in a vain effort to keep his beleaguered spirits up. Paul stood up, glad to be moving away from the sulphurous hole in the room's centre.

He went up to the III door, seeing no clues at all that this could be the right door. His hand reached out and touched the black ring with his pinkie finger. *No point wasting one of the more useful ones,* he thought. He felt no pain, nothing but the cold iron on his skin.

"So are we doing this?" he asked the empty room.

The room did not care to reply in either an affirmative or negative. He was all alone on this decision.

He reached out with his right hand, but then drew it back, deciding to use his weaker left hand instead. He swallowed hard, even though his mouth felt dry, and grasped the metal ring that acted as the door handle. It felt cool against his skin and he loved the tactile feel of the ridges in the metal.

"Okay, on three then," he said, but did the counting in his head for some reason. *Three, two, one!*

He went to pull and then stopped at the very last moment.

"Maybe it knows my lucky number, maybe it's a trap, like the floor. Seven-sided room, six-sided room." He muttered as he edged around the walls to another door. Grabbed the black handle and pulled it inwards, stepping back so the door shielded him from any spike traps or other nasty surprises. Nothing shot out. No sounds were heard.

Paul peeked around the edge of the red door and raised his eyebrows in shock. Remembering to breathe, he peered at what lay beyond the V door. It was a forest at night. The smell of pine and damp leaves entered his nostrils. There was a cool breeze that was gentle, but made him do up his jacket with the two buttons remaining. Paul wasn't sure if this was the right exit, but it sure felt better than fire and brimstone. He walked through the doorway, the damp leaves soaking his socks in seconds. He heard a barn owl hoot to his left and turned to see if he could spot it. When he turned around, he found that the open door had now vanished, leaving only a thick pine tree where he had passed through.

"I was expecting a small polygon-shaped room," he whispered. He wasn't sure why he had lowered his voice. Maybe because he wasn't in an enclosed room anymore and he did not know what terrors the forest held for him.

He moved forwards into a clearing. A full moon was visible through the tree canopy. It gave the trees and the forest floor a silvery glow. He moved into the moonbeams. The place seemed familiar. He moved gingerly over the damp leaves, towards a darker slope across the clearing.

A distant cry of a fox scared him and then he realised it was the first animal he had heard since he had died. He was three feet up the rising slope when he heard another sound. A sound that froze him to the spot as he strained to hear it. It was growing closer. He peered through the gloom to see that the slope levelled off about nine feet above him.

A road?

A vehicle with roaring engine and music blaring out came round a corner above him. Bright headlamps splashed white light through the trees. There was a screech like some primordial beast being taken down by a larger predator and then a crash as the vehicle came flying off the road no more than five feet away. It hit a tree and then rolled three times before crashing into a pine.

Paul scrambled down the bank. The first licks of flame began to show through the windows of the car. The door of the car opened and a figure crawled out onto the grass. For a moment it was anonymous, hidden in the dark of the night, and then a flicker of light crossed the face of the person: Sam.

CHAPTER FORTY-NINE

Sam looked over his shoulder. He kicked out at the creature behind him. The fact that it still looked like Paul made it difficult. "You're not my brother," he hissed. Paul—or the Paul-faced thing—grinned at him and tightened its grip on his ankle. Sam felt the bones of his ankle grind together and the pain shot up his leg and into his hip. He tried to kick again but his foot clattered uselessly against the stone floor.

Behind the creature, flames licked at the open door and paint bubbled up under the heat. Sam realised he should be frightened but the only emotion he recognised was anger. This wasn't Paul! The sacrilege of the creature to dress itself up like his dead brother was too terrible to ignore. Paul was lying in a grave somewhere, mouldering away. He understood that now. He now understood that from the moment he had woken up in the coffin and began his search for his twin brother something—the Great Cremator—had been playing with him, luring him forward with the promise of reuniting him with his lost twin. It was a primal need—an urge to make two halves whole again. Who could tell how deep it ran in him, except whatever had lured him to this point had used that bond to drag him through this hell.

"You tricked me," Sam said.

The creature did not respond. It still looked like Paul; it had the same wiry hair and even the glint of devilment in its eye that their mother had said was Paul's saving grace when it came to girls and the police, but it wasn't Paul.

He stopped struggling.

The creature looked at him, as if it was not sure how to deal with this development.

"You're not my brother."

It opened its mouth to say something. Sam caught sight of a black tongue. "Go on then," Sam challenged him. "Say something."

The creature stood up, its hand still wrapped around Sam's ankle. Its arm stretched. The sight caused Sam's stomach to flip. It was impossible. Unnatural. Something had taken Paul's arm and stretched it like cheap rubber.

"I am the Great Cremator," the creature said. Its voice was low and rumbled around the room.

Sam wanted to say something back—Who died and made you God?—but he was too afraid. The anger had bled away, leaving only confusion. He was in an alien land and he knew none of the rules. Hell, he didn't even know who he was playing against. This was Paul's area—Paul had always known what to do and Sam had been happy to follow behind; the younger brother bringing up the rear. In that moment he yearned for Paul, a deep ache within him that hurt more than he could bear.

"Paul," he whispered. "Come and help me. Save me."

The Great Cremator smiled. It was an ugly grin that didn't fit Paul's mouth. The skin stretched and then split to expose that black tongue and broken teeth around its crooked lips.

"Don't you understand?" it whispered. "He can't save you. Not now. No one can save you."

Despair rolled over Sam like a breath of hot air. Enveloping him. Sam understood—the only thing left to do was to roll over. Take his licks, as Paul used to say when they stood in front of their father waiting for punishment. Because it was true. No one could save him. Whatever other lies the creature spoke through Paul's mouth, this at least was honest. This was how it had always been—even when Paul had been alive, even when they had been so close that it felt they breathed the same breath and the same heart pushed blood through both of their bodies. No one could save him. Not his parents. Not his teachers. Not Paul.

"No one," Sam said quietly.

The Great Cremator looked over its shoulder to the door of the furnace.

Was that how this was supposed to end? Sam wondered. Almost certainly. The creature dragging him across the stone floor and into the furnace. It felt unfair. What had he done to deserve this? He hadn't been evil; he'd hardly had the opportunity to be bad. He was just a boy who'd lived a little too close to the edge at times, but nothing that would warrant the treatment he was receiving.

He put his hands down on the ground, his palms flat against the cool surface. His fingernails scratched against the smooth stones. He decided that when the Great Cremator dragged him down into the bowels of hell he would not cry and he would not scream. He would go to his fate with dignity. That was all he had left. That was the only thing he could offer Paul.

"No, not for Paul, for me," he said. "Because it won't make any difference to Paul now. It won't make any difference to anyone but me."

The creature pulled on his ankle and Sam felt his backbone scrape against the stone floor. Despite his promise, he cried out in terror.

Tears rose from his eyes but dried on his cheeks from the heat of furnace.

"I can't help you," the creature said in Paul's voice. "You have to help yourself."

The stench of his own burning hair filled his senses. The stone floor passed beneath him and he turned on his side to look in the direction that he was being pulled. The doorway was huge and filled with yellow and red flames that left brown scorch marks in the paint. The monster still wore Paul's face, but the skin hung from his chin as if it was melting off the bone.

Sam wanted to kick out but he didn't have the energy. The heat stole any rebellion he felt.

He got closer to the edge of the room, until the soles of his feet passed through the doorway and the smell of burning leather joined the other stink.

He was staring up at the ceiling of the room. Except it wasn't the ceiling—the plaster was gone and instead he saw a metal surface. It looked familiar but his mind was unable to make the connection. The dark red paint of the ceiling was illuminated by the flame from the burning room behind him. One burst of light picked out a patch of rust that looked like the outline of Australia. The light retreated but a moment later it returned and with it the rust became clearer.

I know that stain, Sam thought. He welcomed the distraction, even if it was only for a moment. He inspected the rust and it grew clearer as the flames of the fire grew brighter around him.

He struggled to breathe. Oxygen burnt out of the air around him. The world was getting smaller. The room was now a box that hemmed him in on all sides. *Like a coffin,* Sam thought, although he dismissed the idea as soon as it rose. He'd been in a coffin; this wasn't the same thing at all.

But the space was narrow, and when he reached out, his fingertips brushed against a hard, hot surface. He jerked back his fingers but too late to avoid the sensation of burning that raced up through his hand.

The metal ceiling was just a few inches above him. The scratched map of Australia was as large as his hand. He dropped his head. Now he could no longer move his body, as if he were held in a tight embrace. He struggled against the restraints but they held fast.

When he looked ahead of him, his view of the room had been replaced by darkness. Flames lit up the inside of the car but beyond the shattered glass of the window there was only night. He saw tongues of fire reflected in the fragments of glass that remained. He saw his own face. A younger face. Sam Wright as a nineteen-year-old youth.

Realisation hit him like a hammer blow. The car. He was in the car. He thrashed against the seat belt that held him in place and when it refused to move, he floundered for the release mechanism that lay somewhere beside his hip. He felt the plastic—soft from the heat of the burning car—and tried to release the clip, but it was jammed.

He screamed, "Paul!" and for a second he was in two places at the same time: he was trapped inside the car praying for his brother to save him and yet he was standing on the wet road, shielding his eyes against the flames and beaten back from the heat. He was Sam and he was Paul. Paul and Sam.

"Help me," he screamed.

This isn't how it happened, his mind insisted. *It was Paul who was trapped inside the car. It was Paul who died.*

His throat tightened but it was impossible to tell if it was from the smoke or the memory of the noose he slipped around his neck.

He smelled his own burning flesh. He heard the flames roaring in his ears as the car was consumed.

CHAPTER FIFTY

"Sam," Paul cried as his brother stumbled towards the fire that was spreading through the car. *He must be dazed, concussed,* Paul though. "Sammy!"

Sam did not seem to hear him. Maybe a burning car with your twin inside was slightly more important than him.

"Sam?" Paul said again in a lower voice. He stopped just three yards behind his brother, watching him bend down and peer into the twisted car. Paul's stomach flipped as he looked in at the scene of his own body hanging unconscious in the car.

Sam straightened up and walked around to the rear of the crashed vehicle. Sam looked right past him like he wasn't there. The side of the car was on fire, giving Sam the opportunity to reach into the open boot and pull something out. Paul moved to within a yard of his brother. Sam turned around and moved to the front of the car again.

He completely ignored me, or didn't see me.

Paul rushed over to the side of his twin just as Sam was taking the cap off a red plastic petrol can.

"SAM!" Paul shouted, almost screaming his lungs right into his brother's ear.

It brought no response from his sibling. Sam let the cap dangle down as he began pouring petrol over the front of the car. Over the cracked windscreen, bonnet, and wheels and around to the passenger side wedged against a pine tree. He threw the empty petrol can into the woods, stepped back ten paces, and waited for the inevitable to happen.

"What the fuck are you doing?" Paul cried out as he rushed at his brother. He flew through his twin and landed hard on the damp forest floor. Paul shook his head and turned to look at his brother. Sam had not moved an inch in response. He grabbed at his brother's leg, but his hand passed through it like he was a ghost. Paul stood up and looked at his brother from the side. The flames were running along the bodywork towards the front. Sam did nothing.

No, that wasn't true: he began to smile.

Paul ran over to the burning car. He could see his own body slumped against the seat belt. Smoke had already taken him into unconsciousness. Fire was breaking through from the rear.

What could he do? This had already happened, but without the petrol can pantomime; he was sure. Then there was a blur in his other self's face. A face inside his, mouthing for help. Paul blinked hard three times. Was the smoke playing tricks with his eyes? No, there it was again, the face within his face. A face he knew and brought a whole new level of confusion to the situation. It was Sam's face. It was Sam inside the car now, not him. A hand reached out an inch from where the other former Paul's one lay broken on his lap.

Paul reached out, but a whoosh of oxygen-burning flame leapt up between them. He could not hear Sam's voice, but could see the open-mouthed fear in his blurred face. Paul took a deep breath and reached towards this brother. He hoped his ghostly existence also extended to fire. He reached through, feeling nothing but a cold heat around his wrist. His fingers went through the solid skin and bones like they were made from gas. Yet half an inch below, he found purchase. A hand in his hand. He gripped it hard and it gripped him back. Paul leant back and pulled with all his might. He held his dead breath for one … two … three seconds as he took the strain. Then Sam's spirit came flying out of his burning corpse. Paul fell backwards, with Sam's body falling upon his. They hugged close, reunited once again, in the afterlife.

Yet they did not hit the forest floor.

They landed on a grey stone floor, still in each other's arms. Smiling like loons.

"You saved me," Sam croaked.

"Well, somebody has to," Paul joked and hugged his brother tightly.

"Is ... is it really you?" Sam asked, moving off his brother to kneel beside him.

Paul sat up resting on one elbow. "Who else would it be?"

"I dunno, I've seen a lot of shit since I've been..." Sam's speech faltered.

"Since you've been dead."

"Fake images of you, trying to tempt me, all sorts," Sam said looking down at his knees. Paul scrambled to his feet and reached down a hand to his brother.

"Well, I'm here now, your annoying older and much more handsome brother."

"In ya fucking dreams," Sam said looking up at his brother. He did not take his hand. "I'm sorry that I let you die."

"Me too, but we are both in the same boat now, Bruv, no use wasting the afterlife on regrets. Now get your arse up off the floor." Paul extended his hand a few more inches towards Sam's face.

Sam took it and let his big brother pull him up into a bear hug. "Where the hell are we?"

Paul eyes flicked around the room. He was standing on a cold stone floor in a five-sided room. The room was small with no walls—just five arches with wooden doors. They had a veiled blackness in them, and as Paul looked around there were no numbers below or above them.

"Trapped in the chapel maze again," Paul replied. "But at least we are trapped together now."

CHAPTER FIFTY-ONE

Sam flicked his brother on the nose. "Just checking."

"Checking what? That you're as thick as always?" Paul asked.

Sam felt the grin on his cheeks, but he didn't need a mirror to know what he looked like because the expression was there on Paul's face, too—the pair of them beaming like loons.

"This isn't real," he said. "It can't be."

"You'd rather be stuck down some hole with the worms eating you up? I'm sure it could be arranged."

Sam flicked his brother again. He laughed; they both did. The soft thunk of his fingernails against skin reminded him of arguments when they were kids—of complaining to their mother that *Sam is pinching me* or *Paul just kicked me under the table*.

"We can't stand here waiting for someone to find us," Paul said.

Someone? The Great Cremator. Sam checked behind him but the wooden door was gone. He wondered whether the fiery pit still existed behind one of the doors, like the booby prize in a celestial game show. He imagined opening the door onto a furnace that burnt his eyebrows away in the second it took to gaze down upon the flames. And after his eyebrows would go, his eyelashes and then the skin from his nose and his cheeks, and then the muscle underneath until there was nothing left except bone.

He turned to his older brother and asked, "What do we do now?"

"We get out of this hole."

As simple as that, Sam thought. *We open the door and walk out of the chapel and put the whole mess behind us.* Somehow it didn't feel like it was going to be that easy. The Great Cremator did not strike him as someone who took kindly to losing.

Paul stepped to the door closest to him and placed his ear against the wood.

"What can…"

"Sssh!" Paul hissed. "I'm trying to listen."

Sam watched his brother's face for clues. He stood in the centre of the room, *what do I do?* and realised he'd spent all of his life waiting for Paul to tell him what to do next; he was damned if he was going to spend his afterlife the same way. He crossed to a door opposite from Paul and leaned against the wood. Against the cool of the air, the door felt warm to the touch. Sam placed his hand flat on the surface. Definitely warm. He placed his ear on the wood and tried to hear what might be happening in the room beyond. It was strange, like listening to voices underwater.

He turned and looked across the room to check on Paul. His brother was immersed in listening, too.

"Paul," he whispered. It struck him that there was no need to be quiet, and yet the room still felt like a church and years of training prevented him from shouting. "Paul," he called again, his whisper louder this time.

Still no response. Sam returned to his own door. It was hard to decide where the sound he was hearing actually came from. There were voices buried deep in the mix but that wasn't the only thing. He concentrated, picking apart the different sounds presented to him.

Something mechanical, like huge gears grinding together. It made him think of millstones slowly turning.

He wiped the sweat away from his brow. When he moved from the door, he left an imprint of himself on the wood that quickly dried, like a ghost fading away. *Is that us?* He wondered. *Is that what we are now?*

From the other side of the room his brother made no sound.

"What do you hear?" Sam asked, but received no reply.

He leaned into the door again and the noise returned to

him—voices, the crunch of machinery and … something else. Crackling and snapping and popping. Like… Like…

"Fire!" Sam shouted. He jumped back from the door and turned to Paul. "It's fire!" The look on his brother's face suggested that he had come to the same conclusion. They met in the middle of the stone room. Too late, Sam realised what he had found odd about the place in which they had been trapped: there were no windows.

And why would you put windows inside a furnace?

Paul's face was bright red and his forehead was spotted with pearls of sweat. Sam assumed that he probably looked the same. Saltwater trickled down his brow and stung his eyes. Even when he wiped it away with the back of his hand, it returned almost immediately.

Paul started scratching at the door behind him. "We need to get out of here." The air had the sweet tang of warm flesh and Sam wondered how long it would take until the scent changed from warm flesh to burning skin.

There was a low, long sound. Stones grinding together. Bones grinding together. The whole chamber shook and dust fell down from the ceiling.

"We can't get out," Sam said. His voice was tight and he didn't know whether that was the rarefied atmosphere inside the furnace or simply sheer panic.

"I'm not giving up now," Paul said.

Sam crossed the room until he stood beside Paul. Maybe it was just his imagination, but it hurt just to keep his eyes open. It felt like sand scratching his eyeballs and burrowing into the socket to irritate the soft skin behind his eyes.

The noise of the fire was louder now—a deep roaring, like a giant's bellow, that filled his ears. He could see Paul trying to say something, but it was impossible to hear above the noise. He put a hand on his brother's arm, his skin soft so that it felt like there were no bones in there. He took his brother's hand into his own, sweaty palm to sweaty palm, and turned toward the door behind them.

The sound of machinery rose an octave; there was desperation in the tone. And then the door began slowly to open.

CHAPTER FIFTY-TWO

Both brothers, gripping each other's hands, closed their eyes for possibly the last time. Fire. It was always fire.

Paul thought of Cookie and François, and what terrible things had happened to them. Death upon death, suffering upon suffering. How much more could they take? Paul was ready for the end now, tired of an afterlife of nothing to do but recall the past. At least Sam was at his side this time: hand in hand, waiting for the end of days.

The fire from the open doors was hot against his exposed skin. He felt it tighten against the heat. Sam felt the heat, too, enveloping him, but not burning him. A warm breeze settled around the twins and they opened their eyes at the same split second. No flames had entered the room. They stared through the open doors onto a corridor of brown stone that stretched into the darkness before them. Red shadows flicked around it, with huge cogs the size of Ferris wheels slowly turning and grinding. Flames burst out in gusts from somewhere below them.

"Forwards?" Sam pointed.

"Looks like it, brother," Paul said.

They gripped each other's hands tighter and walked through the doors into the cavernous nightmare beyond. The outlines of the walls were rocky seams of black and red, like a huge subterranean cathedral. The brown stone path was a walkway, like a tall waterless aqueduct with spanned arches plunged hundreds of feet deep into a fiery lava lake below. Fire bursts shot up from below, illuminating for the first time the full evil nature of the vast cavern.

"Oh Jesus," Paul heard Sam whisper, as they saw the machinery in its full glory for the first time. A body fell from high above. A woman, with long blonde hair streaming around her head. She looked very much like a teacher, Miss McHenry, he and Sam had in their first year in senior school. They had both had a massive crush on her and dropped many pencils, just for a glimpse of her thighs that year. Below her were linked copper chains with a ring at the top. Miss McHenry fell down into them and only then did her screaming really start.

The clothes were ripped from her body. Red slashes appeared in her exposed flesh. As the chains funnelled downwards Paul saw that the inside of the chain was lined with barbed hooks that stripped away clothing, skin, and hair.

Miss McHenry was nothing more than a red, raw mess as she finally passed through the chains. She landed between two cogs, each a hundred and sixty feet wide and twenty feet thick. Paul prayed she was already dead, but when the cogs crushed her feet and ankles together, her screams echoed throughout the cavern. Her bones were reduced to red soup. Only when the cogs broke her ribs and crushed her lungs did she stop screaming.

The twin brothers looked away as the remains of their old teacher slopped downwards to be consumed in the fires below.

"Run," Sam suddenly urged, and Paul took up that charge. They hurried along the stone bridge, trying not to take in what their vision was showing them. The cavern seemed endless. The darkness ahead was filled with red cogs turning death. They slowed to a jog now, knowing they could do nothing but press onwards.

"Sam … Paul!" Someone wailed over the crescendo of noise. The twins skidded to a halt. A dark-haired girl was hanging from the middle of her chain. She was bloodied and half dressed in ripped jeans and a blood-splattered white blouse. One of the barbed hooks had gone through her left palm and stopped her deathly descent. She dangled a hundred feet above them.

"Hana Kadivar," Paul said in a low astonished voice. They had gone to school with her. Her family had escaped Iran and they had come to England where Hana's uncle already lived.

Both the boys had fancied her rotten. When she left for college, Hana had been forced into an arranged marriage and they never saw her again.

"Hana," Sam called up to her, "hang on."

"How the hell do we help her?" Paul said. The bridge along the centre of the cavern was thirty feet away from the cogs and she was high above them.

"We'll find a way to help you!" Sam called up to her as she struggled to hang on.

"How the fuck are we going to do that?" Paul hissed in a low voice to his brother. "Got a cherry-picker in your funeral suit pocket?"

They looked up to the dangling Hana in despair. Then another body fell from the darkness. The twins watched as the fat man hit her, ripping her hand from the chain and sending her down into the cogs. Both fell into the machine, squashed together like two different colours of play dough.

Paul put his arm around his brother and pulled him away from the awful sight.

CHAPTER FIFTY-THREE

Sam pushed himself away from Paul and looked down even though he knew his brother was right to try and hide it from him.

The fat man … he'd seen him before. There was not enough of the man's face left for him to recognise him from the pulp of raw meat that now squeezed between the cogs of the infernal machine, but he held on to the image he had of the man's face, his mouth wide open in a scream of perfect agony, before the cogs had rolled together to crush him.

He tried to concentrate. It seemed important to remember who the fat man had been, but Hana's screams made it impossible. Part of him wanted to scream at her: *Just hurry up and die!* And although the realisation flooded him with guilt, it didn't make the thought any less true. Then he had it, only when the fat man was gone. He had taught him and his brother to drive, with varying degrees of success, taking into consideration the cause of Paul's demise.

Then he remembered that he'd had a crush on Hana.

Sam laughed, a high, braying noise that tipped over the edge into hysteria. It wasn't even funny. It was sick.

A crush. On Hana.

He laughed until it hurt, and even then he couldn't stop. His throat was sore and it was getting harder to breathe, and yet he couldn't stop the laughter that overwhelmed him.

This is who you are.

He wasn't sure if the words came from inside him, or if they were spoken by someone else. He looked across at his brother—this was who they were. They were the killers. They were the selfish bastards. How could it not be true? Sam thought of all the people that had tried to help him, from the moment he had woken up in the coffin. All of them dead because of him. And hadn't Paul said something similar? About friends he had acquired and then discarded. And now Hana and the fat man that he didn't even care enough about to remember his name were both dead.

He looked down past the machinery to the lava below. *Jump.* The idea was attractive. There would be no return from the fires, nothing left to package in a neat coffin for him to rise from once more. There would just be a moment's heat and then oblivion.

Another body fell from the darkness. She flashed past and landed on one of the cogs. *Trish.* Her clothes were aflame, and even as he watched, her skin began to bubble and blacken with the heat. She writhed on the metal edge of the cog, and by the way she moved, Sam thought her back had been broken by the impact. And then she turned and saw him.

"Help me!"

Her voice should not have carried so far. Not with the roar of the furnace to drown it, and yet he heard her perfectly. "Help me."

He heard the grinding of the wheels and then felt the movement shudder up through the stone bridge. The woman scrabbled against the cog, trying to stay away from the point where the cogs met, but it was a fruitless attempt. As the teeth joined together over her arm and dragged her down into the body of the machine, the woman let out a terrible scream that seemed to Sam to be a perfect cry of pain. He looked away from his guilt.

A man stood at the end of the bridge where a moment before there had only been broiling air. No, not a man, a boy. *The* boy. Sam opened his mouth to speak, but before he could say anything a second figure joined the first. A tall, black woman with a suede waistcoat and silver hotpants.

He heard Paul whisper a single word: "Cookie?" Sam looked at the woman again—she looked to be a lot of things, but Cookie wouldn't have been high on his list of descriptions. No, she was too strong for that. And yet Paul whispered the name again, "Cookie, is that really you?"

The boy and the woman started to walk across the stone bridge. Side by side, although the bridge did not seem wide enough to accommodate both of them.

As they moved closer, the height differential between them lessened. The woman grew shorter or the boy grew taller, Sam wasn't sure which, and yet in truth it was neither of those two things. They simply converged on a height that was neither one nor the other.

"Who are you?" Sam asked.

The woman spoke, and yet the voice was that of the small boy. "We are the Great Cremator." The thick, purple makeup bleached from her lips until they were pale pink. The boy's face altered and his eyelashes grew into long, false lashes thick with mascara.

"Cookie?" Paul asked. And finally Sam understood. Cookie—the woman who had helped him through the land of the dead. Cookie and the boy, together. He was sure it was not a coincidence. Nothing since the moment he had woken up trapped in his coffin had been a coincidence.

"Cookie, what are you doing?" Paul asked.

It was the boy who spoke, with a soft New York drawl that Sam assumed was the voice of Cookie. "We are the Great Cremator."

They stopped halfway down the bridge. Heat from the pits below rose up and twisted the air and melted everything so that Cookie became the boy and the boy became Cookie until there was not two people standing on the bridge in front of them but just one—an amalgam of the pair. If Sam stared at the figure hard enough, he could pick out elements of the boy's face or recognise a patch of Cookie's silver hotpants fused into the boy's brown trousers. It hurt to look too long. It hurt trying to pull apart the two people into separate entities once more.

"Is this who you were all along?" Sam asked. The image of the boy immersed in the fire came back to him. At the time he had been destroyed with guilt, certain that the boy's death was his fault. And yet now with hindsight he replayed the scene and remembered that it had been the boy's choice to give himself up to the fire.

The face of the person in front of him stretched until it was no longer the boy, no longer Cookie. It was a new individual. Features rose up from beneath the flesh as if revealing an individual who had been there all along. A man in his early fifties, salt-and-pepper hair thinning at the sides and deep wrinkles that creased his face with character. The Great Cremator. Sam didn't feel that he needed an introduction.

He wore a black three-piece suit. Small black eyes like ball bearings peered out at the twins from the pits of his eye sockets, and at the heart of each eye was a fleck of red/yellow flame.

"What do you want?" Paul asked.

Sam didn't dare turn away from the Great Cremator to look at his brother. He felt that if he dropped his concentration for a fraction of a second, he would be lost. But he wanted to look at Paul, to see if he could find where the strength came from. He was sure his brother was afraid, and yet his voice was solid and strong and spoke for both of them.

"Whatever it is, we're not playing," Paul said.

"I am all of the dead. I led you here, giving you just enough hope to carry you to me," the fiend laughed. "All the suffering of the dead is down to you; this has been your private hell, fuelled by the dead that you knew in life. Now you are here, trapped in the belly of the beast. I caught your companions and sliced and diced them into a fine spray of blood and snorted them up my nose. It was a great high. Now you are here inside the deep inner workings of my leviathan. There is no escape, no life, nothing but your empty sad souls and what I deem to do with them over eternity."

"Go to hell," Sam said. He felt his brother move closer to him, their shoulders pressing together. Thick as thieves, their mother had described them on more than one occasion. Sam knew he was grinning—he could feel the muscles on his face pull tight. He leaned against his brother. "Go to hell."

The Great Cremator stood in silence for a moment.

"One of you can leave. One of you must stay. That is my price."

CHAPTER FIFTY-FOUR

"Fuck you and the rancid pony you rode in on, mate," Sam shot back. He'd had enough. He had found his brother and received his forgiveness. Something that he had sought for so long, crushing any dream he'd had of life, happiness, getting married, and kids. It was the tightrope over the cavernous abyss that he had walked every single day since Paul had died. They were together again. Whatever happened, they would face it as one.

"What he said with such aplomb." Paul wrinkled his nose in defiance at the Great Cremator and reached out for Sam's hand. His twin took it instinctively.

"You don't understand what I am offering." The Great Cremator's form changed again. Belching black smoke that filled the width of the bridge and beyond. Wider and higher the smoke rose until they could see nothing but its gigantic shade covering the way forward. Snake-like tendrils wormed through and around its undulating smoky form. Soon there was nothing but his darkness surrounding them and the tiny circle of rock on which they stood against him.

"Neat trick. Who do you think you are? Houdini? The answer is still no. Live, unlive, or die forever, we do it together," Paul bravely shouted up at the thing. Yet his voice died as soon as it hit the Great Cremator.

"Ohh … rhyming, well done," Sam laughed, turning to look at his brother.

"One tries one's best under the circumstances," Paul laughed back in a posh-sounding version of his voice.

The all-encompassing form seemed to quiver in anger. A

voice from nowhere and everywhere bellowed down at them, forcing the twins to kneel against the sonic assault.

"You are nothing. You do not understand the torture I will inflict on you. I will bring everyone you ever loved back to life and kill them over and over again. You will *listen* to ME!"

The bass tones of the Great Cremator pounded the twins. They had to separate their hands to each cover their ears. The twins felt their ribs rattle in their chests as blood trickled from their eardrums.

"Okay, you've got our attention—prick!" Sam shouted over the reverberating echoing din.

"Stop!" Paul wailed against the agonising searing in his head.

Then there was silence.

It took a few seconds for the twins to realise the awful noise had ceased. Their ears were still ringing like the pealing bells of a church on Christmas morning. Then a sound permeated the deafening silence. The crackle of a nearby fire and the faint rustling of leaves on a breeze.

"Do I have your undivided attention now?" The Great Cremator's voice was low, but still deep, like he had smoked Marlboros for a thousand years.

The twins could do little but nod.

"Good. Let me make myself clear. One stays and one goes: your choice. The one who stays, stays for all eternity as part of my legion of dead. The other I will restore to life, to live out their mortal days for a guaranteed ninety more years. All you have to do is decide, who lives and who dies?"

Paul and Sam sat up on their knees, looking at each other. The ground beneath them was damp. As the encompassing darkness of the Great Cremator gave way, they saw tall vertical shapes around them, and a blurred, eye-wincing fire close by.

"What do you think?" Sam asked Paul.

"You should take the deal and get your life back. It seems to me that you didn't have much of one after I died," Paul replied.

"But what about you? You were barely out of short trousers when I killed you. You need this life more than I." Sam felt a delicate wind on his cheek and moisture in the air. The smoky darkness parted to reveal stars and the canopy of trees over their heads. It was nighttime in the woods again. The burning car wedged against the pine tree again. It was a choice of who lived and who died once more.

The two brothers grinned at each other. Paul clapped Sam on the back as they got up off their knees. Once again, they took each other's hands. An understanding passed between them. They were calm, relaxed, and together.

"You sure about this, cause I had sex way more times than you ever did?" Sam smiled broadly at his twin brother.

"In your dreams, brother. Even with all those extra years I still did it more than you," Paul grinned back at his twin. "But yeah—it's the only way."

They squeezed each other's hand and turned to face the Great Cremator's smoky form before them.

"No deal," they said in unison, and hand in hand walked towards the burning wreck.

"What are you doing?" cried the Great Cremator as they headed for the flaming car.

"We aren't quite sure," Sam replied.

"But we are doing it together this time," Paul said as the two brothers walked together into the burning inferno.

MEET THE AUTHORS

PETER MARK MAY is the author of nine horror novels and one novella: *Demon, Kumiho, Inheritance* [as P. M. May], *Dark Waters* (novella), *Hedge End, AZ: Anno Zombie, Something More Than Night, Forky's House, The End of All Flesh Book 1: The Flood* in 2019 and *The End of All Flesh: Book 2: The Red Death* in 2020.

He's had short stories published in genre Canadian & US magazines and UK & US anthologies of horror such as *Creature Feature, Watch,* the British Fantasy Society's 40th Anniversary anthology *Full Fathom Forty, Alt-Zombie, Fogbound From 5, Nightfalls, Demons & Devilry, Miseria's Chorale, The Bestiarum Vocabulum, Phobophobias, Kneeling in the Silver Light, Demonology* and *Tales From the Lake Volume 5.*

He also writes historical crime under the name Alexander Arrowsmith. His first two, *The Athens Atrocities* and *The Medousa Murders,* were published 2019.

He also runs Hersham Horror Books and has published 30 books so far.

Peter's website is: http://petermarkmay.weebly.com/

RICHARD FARREN BARBER was born in Nottingham in July 1970. After studying in London he returned to the East Midlands. He lives with his wife and son and works as a manager for a local university.

He has over 80 short stories in publications including: *Alt-Dead, Alt-Zombie, DarkFuse, ePocalypse—Tales from the End, Fever Dreams, Horror D'Oeuvres, Murky Depths, Midnight Echo, Midnight Street, Morpheus Tales, Night Terrors II, Siblings, The House of Horror, Trembles, When Red Snow Melts,* and broadcast on Tales to

Terrify, Pseudopod, and The Wicked Library.

Richard has six novellas published: *The Power of Nothing, The Sleeping Dead, Odette, Perfect Darkness, Perfect Silence, Closer Still,* and *All Hell.* His debut novel *The Living and the Lost* was published in 2019.

Find him at his website: www.richardfarrenbarber.co.uk

Curious about other Crossroad Press books?
Stop by our site:
http://store.crossroadpress.com
We offer quality writing
in digital, audio, and print formats.

Lightning Source UK Ltd.
Milton Keynes UK
UKHW010627100221
378552UK00001B/204

9 781952 979750